V

The Barbarian
Menderchuck
Paul
Rodenburg

Kal Bartek
Paul
Rodenburg

The Chains of
Belloch
Paul
Rodenburg

WWW.ZANSADVENTURES.COM

THE CHAINS OF BELLOCH

Book 3 of the Menderchuck Saga

by

Paul Rodenburg

The characters and events portrayed in this book are fictitious. Any similarity to real persons, living or dead, is coincidental and not intended by the author.

ISBN: 979-8-218-00002-8

CHAPTER 1: SIZTOK

Vast, if there was a single word that described the Steppes of Rannsaka, then it was Vast. Its vast grasslands stretched in all directions, from distant horizon to distant horizon, like a golden ocean.

Dangerous, if there was a single word that better described the Steppes of Rannsaka, then it was Dangerous. For generations, heavily armed raiders, who were known as the horse clans, had swept through the vast grasslands like wild untamed prairie fires. And though the horse clans were no more, the Steppes remained a most dangerous of places.

Changing, if there was a single word that best described the Steppes of Rannsaka, then it was Changing. A new wind of change blew through the golden stalks of grass that covered its vast dangerous grasslands.

Deep in the heart of the Steppes, where the Grantosh and Golyn rivers met, forming the Greater Golyn, there stood the ancient sprawling city of Siztok. Its thick storied stone walls could be seen from miles away, rising high above the prairie grass that waved and danced in the wind.

The city, like its inhabitants, was deeply divided in two. The city's center was founded upon a wide shallow plateau encircled by an ancient stone wall. Between its walls, in spotless palatial manor homes along cobblestone roads, there lived the city's rich and affluent.

They lounged in great parks filled with elaborate hedge sculptures and surrounded by wrought iron fences. They bathed in opulent bath houses made of marble and gold. They dined in fine restaurants that smelled of roast duck. And they shopped in exotic stores which rested in the lee of the stone wall.

The ancient stone wall had been built long ago in an attempt to protect the city from the multitude of marauding horse raiders who had once inhabited the Steppes. In this, the wall had been very effective, guarding the fortunes of those who had been lucky enough to have been born within its confines. Now, though, the wall was used much more often to keep out the poor of the lower city.

The lower city consisted of all that existed outside of the stone wall. Great sprawling neighborhoods of squat wood huts, connected by putrid dirt roads, spread out from the wall like a claustrophobic spider web of great intricacy. There, among the filth and the grime, lived the great unwashed masses of Siztok.

As the unforgiving noonday sun climbed high into the great blue sky, beating down mercilessly upon the city, a thick suffocating air of fear and uncertainly hung stubbornly over rich and poor alike.

Four days prior, a new city had sprung up over night just outside of Siztok, a city of tents. It was there that Duke Belloch's grand army had made camp. By evening, the army's campfires had lit up the night as though the ground were full of stars. Anxiously, the people of Siztok had looked on at the great horde of foreign invaders.

"Anything from the emissaries?" asked the Lord Mayor in a hushed whisper.

"No, M'lord."

"Ugghhh," sighed the Lord Mayor, running his frustrated hand through his thinning hair. "Very well, if that changes, let me know immediately."

The guard nodded, then turned to leave, carefully closing the room's immense oak doors behind him.

Nervously, the Lord Mayor fidgeted with the golden chain that held the great seal of the city around his portly neck. Then he put on the calm fake face of an experienced politician, smoothed his silk sleeves, and turned towards his guests.

Slowly, the Lord Mayor's heavy footsteps proceeded across the exquisite marble floor, echoing out in the cavernous room as he waddled past gilded paintings and marble sculptures on his way toward the great mahogany table.

There, around the table, sat over a dozen men and women, dressed in fine silks and dainty lace, adorned by gold and silver jewelry. They were the elite rich of Siztok, and they had been summoned to council by the Lord Mayor himself.

Hard decisions, the Mayor reckoned, were best made by a group of people. That way there was always someone to blame if it went bad. Whereas easy decisions were best made alone, so one could keep the credit to themselves.

skreeeetch Echoed out the sounds of the Lord Mayor's chair scraping against the marble floor as he pulled it out and took a seat at the head of the grand table.

"Sorry about the interruption," declared the Lord Mayor with authority. "Now, does anyone have any good ideas about our situation?"

"Maybe," suggested an old man, wearing a navy blue shirt gleaming with silver lace. "Maybe we could find a dragon egg, raise it, and he'd eat the army!"

A few of the assembled nodded in agreement while the Lord Mayor rolled his eyes.

"Do you have a dragon egg?" asked the frustrated Lord Mayor.

"No."

"Do you know where to get a dragon egg?"

"No..."

"Do you have a hundred years to raise and train a dragon?!" snapped the Lord Mayor.

"No..., but other than that, it's a pretty good idea," retorted the old man to a smattering of

4

supportive applause.

"Ugghhhh," groaned the Lord Mayor. "Let's just put a pin in that idea, then. Does anyone have any ideas that don't take a hundred years?"

"What if we just tell them that we're not home?" suggested a young man in a frilly white shirt.

"Yes! Yes! Here! Here!" agreed a number of foppish voices.

"We can just say we moved or something," added the young man with a pride filled smile.

"Firstly! They aren't seeing our messengers," snorted the Lord Mayor. "Secondly, don't you think they'd suspect something when we walked up to them, saying that we moved?"

"Oh," replied the saddened young man. "I hadn't thought of that."

"I still think we need a dragon egg," interrupted the old man.

The Lord Mayor face palmed, talking through gritted teeth, "ANY OTHER IDEAS?"

"Duke's Belloch's army has been camped outside of our town for four days..." began Lady Victoria.

"Duke Belloch's been camped outside for four days," parroted the Lord Mayor in a cruel mimicking voice. "I know that! You know that! Blind babies know it! That doesn't help us!

You're useless. You're all useless!"

Four days earlier, led by the sound of fife and drum, Duke Belloch's massive army had marched to the outskirts of Siztok and made camp. Ominously, they waited, sending no emissaries. Each day, the nervous Lord Mayor had sent dozens of his own emissaries to make parley with the Duke, but all were refused without explanation.

Now the Siztokians were no strangers to invaders. Over the ages, they had weathered raids too numerous to count from the various horse clans. Those, though, were quick affairs with horse raiders rushing in, grabbing what they could carry from the undefended poor of the lower city, and speeding off again. In living memory, Siztok had never experienced an army like Belloch's, one that just sat there, silently waiting.

This was a new kind of psychological warfare that the Duke was waging. He had learned it from his wife. She had called it 'the silent treatment.' He had called it 'hell, on earth.' Panic tore through Siztok while citizens desperately wondered what they had done wrong to deserve such a fate, fearing the horrors that the Duke's silent army would eventually unleash upon them.

"Does anyone have any useful ideas?" despondently inquired the Lord Mayor, playing with his gavel which lay upon the table.

CRASH The great oak doors of the lavish

room burst open.

"Your worship! Your worship!"

"Go away Gene!" snapped the Lord Mayor. "Can't you see we're in the middle of a meeting?!"

"But your worship, I have a message from Duke Belloch himself!"

"Bring it here immediately!" commanded the Lord Mayor, sitting upright in his chair.

Gene sped across the marble floor, paper in hand, until he had reached the Lord Mayor.

"Give it here! Give it here!" grunted the Lord Mayor, ripping the paper from the messenger's hand.

The Lord Mayor held the small folded piece of paper, which bore the wax seal of Duke Belloch, before him. Siztok's elite rich and Gene stood there in quiet anxiety, eyes fixed upon the paper.

"Go away Gene!" barked the Lord Mayor. "And shut the door behind you. Go faster!"

Gene rushed out of the room, slamming the great oak doors behind him. As the echo of the doors reverberated loudly throughout the room, the Lord Mayor slipped a finger between the creases of paper, breaking Duke Belloch's seal. Cautiously, he unfolded the paper, glancing down in trepidation at its words. Then he looked up at those assembled around him and began to read the note aloud.

"Surrender and give me the building of my choice in your uptown. Do this, and your mayor may maintain his position and powers, and the rich may keep all that they have. Siztok shall be my seat of government on the plains, and we shall all grow richer due to its increased trade. Refuse, and you know what will happen.

Signed,
Duke Belloch of Rivolli"

"What's that mean?" asked Victoria. "What will happen if we refuse?"

"Don't be dense," grumbled the Lord Mayor, staring at the message in his hand. "We all know what will happen, and it won't be pleasant."

The room filled with the murmur of agreement and the nodding of heads, even though no one was really sure what the Duke's threat actually entailed. The four days of silent treatment had given their imaginations plenty of time to concoct wild visions of the most terrible possible fates.

"Well," declared the Lord Mayor. "That leaves us with two choices. Either we allow the poor into the upper city.."

"Ewww, no," erupted a woman covered in gold jewelry.

"Either we allow the poor into the upper city," repeated the Lord Mayor with a scowl at having been interrupted. "And together we hold out as long as we can, or we open the gates and surrender to Duke Belloch's demands, knowing that our fortunes are secure. In fact, we may all grow richer."

"What about the poor though?" asked Victoria, clutching her diamond necklace. "Won't someone think of the poor?"

A roomful of annoyed eyes turned towards her.

"Because I won't," added Victoria, a devilish grin spreading across her face.

Like a sharp needle puncturing a full balloon, Victoria's words popped the oppressive anxiety which hung over all assembled. A great torrent of laughter erupted from the Lord Mayor and the elite rich around him.

"Excellent!" smiled the Lord Mayor. "Then it is agreed. For the good of us... er... the entire city of Siztok, we shall surrender immediately."

"Wait," interrupted Victoria. "Wait, I need time to make my idiot children and my boorish husband presentable. After all, first impressions are everything."

A low rumble of agreement spread like wildfire throughout the room.

"Yes, yes, good point," agreed the Lord Mayor. "One hour, in one hour we shall surrender. Until then, get out your finest apparel, so that we may make a good impression on our new lords.

And no matter what, DO NOT tell your servants about any of this. The poor must not know until it's over. Meeting adjourned."

No sooner had the Lord Mayor banged his gavel to conclude the meeting, then the rich around him instantly leapt to their feet, rushing from the room.

CHAPTER 2: THE DUKE'S WILL

Timidly, a young peasant boy watched the massive halted column of heavily armed foreign invaders. Brightly, their armor shone beneath the sunlight like a gigantic blue snake covered in silver scales. Grimly silent, the multitude of blue uniformed soldiers stood at attention, stretching from the city's outskirts, snaking up through the dilapidated crooked streets of Siztok's lower quarters, and ending just short of the upper city's main gate.

At the head of the column in the shadow of the great gate's wooden doors, sitting upon a white stallion that was almost as pristine as his royal blue tunic, Duke Belloch patiently waited. Calmly, he rested a riding glove clad hand upon his sword's golden hilt. Sitting beside him upon a brown horse, wearing a leather jerkin upon his body and a curved saber upon his hip, was his henchman, Oleg. Nervously, Oleg fidgeted with his horse's reigns.

"I don't know, boss," whispered Oleg, warily eyeing the town's archers who stood guard atop the high stone wall before them. "This might be a trap."

"Oh?" replied the Duke, slightly raising an eyebrow.

"Look at them up there. If this is a trap, they could start raining arrows down on us at any moment."

"Oh, my simple friend," grimly smiled the Duke.

"We're friends?" excitedly interrupted Oleg.

"No, of course not," scoffed the Duke to Oleg's sudden disappointment. "I'm assuming your quaint horse clans never could breach this wall."

Oleg nodded slowly in embarrassed agreement, "A few times Menderchuck spurred us on, in a vain attempt to cross the gates before they closed, but we never succeeded."

"And where is Menderchuck now?" asked the Duke like a patronizing parent.

"Dead," lied Oleg, as he had many times before. "Slain by my hand in battle long ago."

"Exactly, and anyways, my people are not morons like your people were," coldly added the Duke. "If Siztok were to defy us, go back on their surrender acceptance, then we would build great siege engines. We would tear down their wall, brick by brick, then tear their inhabitants apart, rendering them limb by limb. But happily, that won't be necessary. Any moment now, that gate will open and the upper city will be ours."

Almost as though on cue, the massive wooden doors of the gate swung open with a great creak, revealing the opulent splendor of the upper city. Oleg's eyes grew wide with surprise, witnessing the great eager crowds, who were dressed in their finest, that lined both sides of the wide cobble stone street.

Then a short corpulent man, who wore a shining chain around his neck which bore the gold seal of Siztok, stepped out from the throngs of the assembled rich. Boldly, he strolled toward Duke Belloch, carrying a parchment in one hand. As he approached, the corpulent man bent over in a great flourishing bow. As he rose, he lifted the parchment to his eyes and began to read aloud.

"Hear ye! Hear ye! As Lord Mayor of the grand city of Siztok and its associated municipalities, including, but not limited to, the muddy eel banks of the East Golyn and the dung heaps beyond, I do hereby declare that the grand city of Siztok officially surrenders to the glorious conqueror of the Steppes himself, Duke Belloch."

A sycophantic cheer erupted from the conquered rich of Siztok.

Confused, wide eyed, Oleg turned toward the Duke and whispered, "Why are they happy to be conquered?"

"Greed Oleg, greed," responded the Duke, spurring his horse lightly forward.

As the Duke's white stallion stepped over the threshold of the great gate and into the upper city proper, the Duke lightly waved to all assembled.

"Your surrender is accepted," declared the Duke to the uproarious applause of the assembled rich.

The Lord Mayor excitedly waddled over to the Duke, bowing low beside his horse.

"Your Lordship, it is a great honor to surrender to your magnificence on this fine day. Thank you, my Lord, for choosing to conquer us, your lowly servants."

"You're welcome," dryly responded Duke Belloch.

"We are all so eager to meet you," added the Lord Mayor, rising from his bow. "With your permission, your Grace, may I present to you, Lady Victoria and her family."

With a toothy smile upon her alabaster face, Victoria eagerly stepped forward.

"It is a great honor to meet the virile, victorious conqueror himself, Duke Belloch," flirted Victoria, waving a diamond encrusted fan before her. "Duke, that is such a majestic title. It just rolls off of your tongue, Duke. Might I, between you and I, call you Duukie?"

Lady Victoria winked seductively at Duke Belloch, who recoiled with a grimace at the sight.

"Lord Mayor," stiffly asked an offended Duke Belloch. "Did she just call me a dookie?"

"No sir! No sir!" floundered the Lord Mayor, turning a deep beet red. "Well... maybe she did sir, she didn't mean it like that though. Forgive her, she was dropped on her head as a child...

many times."

"I WAS NOT...UmPh..." grunted Lady Victoria as the Lord Mayor punched her in the gut, silencing her dispute mid-sentence.

"Perhaps, your lordship, you would like a tour of the upper city?" groveled the Mayor, recovering his composure.

"No," sneered the Duke, glancing derisively at the town around him. "I'm afraid I've already seen too much. That big building, up yonder, what is it?"

The Lord Mayor's eyes traced the trail from the Duke's pointing finger tip, up the cobble stone street, to a massive cathedral which dominated the upper city.

"Why that's St. Ufstath's cathedral," beamed the Lord Mayor. "It is our pride and joy. A living monument to the saint himse..."

"Excellent," rudely interrupted the Duke. "It will do. That will be my new capital building."

"But... but, but, sir," stammered the Mayor. "That's holy ground. The monks live there..."

"Are you going back on our deal?" asked the Duke in a voice tinged with threat.

"No... No sir! Excellent choice for your new capital M'Lord. Would you like me to notify the monks of their eviction?"

"No need," dismissed Duke Belloch.

CHAPTER 3: THE NEW CAPITAL

According to legend, St. Ufstath had been a humble itinerant preacher who had eschewed the comforts of modern life. With only the ragged robes upon his body and his trusty walking stick at his side, he had braved the hardships of the world, healing and ministering to the poor on his travels.

And so the modern monks of St. Ufstath's cathedral vowed to live in the holy saint's image... more or less. They had quickly done away with the concept of ragged robes. They were much too cold and embarrassing to wear. Traveling from town to town also seemed to be a major inconvenience, so that too had to go. And it turns out that braving the hardships of the world was also rather unpleasant. Instead, the monks built a lavish cathedral to honor their favored saint. From their saintly monument, they could minister to the citizens of the upper city by gratefully taking their offerings.

Like a black stone mountain made by man, the monstrously large base of St. Ufstath's cathedral emerged from the pristine ground of Siztok's upper city, dwarfing all around it in ostentatious splendor

Even Sybox, the world's greatest known mountain climber, would have found great difficulty in attempting to ascend the massive black stone blocks that formed the cathedral's outer walls. Any journey upward would have consisted of days of sweaty backbreaking work, climbing past great stained glass windows, pausing to make camp amongst the multitude of marble statues of various saints which stood on ledges high above, and grappling great stone gargoyles before finally reaching the twin summits which attempted to pierce the heavens high above.

The twin summits, which were lavish bell towers of immense size, were only visited once a week. In the middle of each week, two unfortunate monks would be chosen for bell tower duty. The first monk would begin the lonely trek up the great internal stairway that lead to the summit of the first bell tower, while the second monk would mirror his actions in the second tower.

For two whole days, these monks would laboriously climb in quiet solitude. On the morning of the third day, each would emerge into their respective bell tower, beholding the tower's great bell with weary amazement. Most would then gaze across the massive chasm that separated the two bell towers, calling out a greeting to their fellow monk, the first person that they had seen in days. Then they would complete their sacred duty by ringing St. Ufstath's cathedral's two great bells in unison, announcing the call to services.

Duke Belloch stood before the steps of the grand cathedral while the Lord Mayor, Oleg, and two companies of the Duke's soldiers quietly looked on. Curious, the Duke arched his neck backward, gazing up at the bright shining gold roofed twin bell towers that soared high above.

"Yes, yes," remarked the Duke, smiling to himself. "This will do. Oleg, open the doors."

Doubtfully, Oleg looked up at the great twin oak doors that dominated the church's front face.

"Help me boys," demanded Oleg, gesturing toward a nearby bench.

Obediently, a handful of soldiers broke ranks, placing their hands upon the bench.

"One, two, three," grunted Oleg as the small group of men lifted the bench and then began to advance menacingly upon the church's grand doors.

"What in the world are you doing?" asked the Duke with a quizzical look upon his face.

"Battering ram," grunted Oleg.

"No, no, no, you will do no such thing. Look at that door, it is a work of supreme craftsmanship."

"That's a good eye you have there, your Grace," groveled the Lord Mayor.

"Of course it is," dismissed the Duke. "Now Oleg, stop being silly. Put that bench down. I will not have you damaging the doors of my new capital building."

Instantly, Oleg released his end of the bench, causing it to crash down upon the feet of a nearby soldier who howled out in pain.

"Then how do we get in?" asked Oleg, gesturing toward the door.

"Try knocking," sighed the Duke, who then turned toward the Lord Mayor. "I swear, he's helpless without me."

With an indifferent shrug, Oleg crossed the cobblestone street. Heavily, he leapt up the church's front stairs, pausing for the briefest of moments, then slamming his fist into the door, knocking three times. All stood in silent anticipation, eyes glued to the massive church doors.

"You want that I should knock again?" called out Oleg, glancing back over his shoulder towards Duke Belloch.

It was then that Oleg heard a slow creaking sound. As he turned back toward the doors, he found himself face to face with an elderly face.

"A homeless man, in the upper city?" gasped the elderly abbot, staring at Oleg. "Don't let the Lord Mayor know that you've sneaked up here or he'll have you clapped in irons. You've caught us at a bad time. We are in the middle of our supper. Come back in an hour, and we shall share our leftovers with you."

CRAAACK

"OWWWW!" cried out the old abbot, reeling backwards, grasping his face in pain, sporting a red bruise upon his face that strongly resembled Oleg's fist.

Rudely, Oleg pushed the church doors open wide.

"Let's clean it out boys," ordered Oleg, stepping into the church proper.

Two companies of Duke Belloch's soldiers, weapons drawn, charged into the cathedral. In very short order, a series of terrified shrieks and pain filled screams began to emanate from deep within the church.

"Follow me," instructed the Duke.

With the Lord Mayor in tow, Duke Belloch climbed the cathedral's front stairs and stepped into its hallowed halls.

"Well, these statues need to go," noted Belloch, glancing at the holy effigies which adorned its halls.

Screaming monks, robes bloody and torn, fled past Duke Belloch and the Lord Mayor, pouring out into the street beyond. As the last monk limped by, a charging Oleg kicked him in the buttocks, sending the monk tumbling down the church stairs. Then, with a mighty slam, Oleg sealed the church doors closed behind them.

"Good work, Oleg," commended the Duke. "Now summon my architect. I have a new project for him. You could call it a model project."

Duke Belloch chuckled lightly to himself while his assembled men stared in silence.

"Now.."

knock

"Now," repeated the Duke in slight frustration at having been interrupted.

knock *knock*

"NOW, we need..."

knock *knock* *knock*

"UGH!" blurted out Duke Belloch. "Must I take care of everything myself?!"

Duke Belloch stormed towards the cathedral's front doors, throwing them open. There, standing directly before him upon the church's top stair, was the elderly abbot of St. Ufstath's cathedral.

"What do you want?" demanded the Duke.

"You can't throw us from here," declared the abbot. "This is a house of god, and our home. We are, but his humble servants."

The Duke stared silently at the abbot.

"And... Well..." continued the abbot with growing conviction. "You see, we listen to the will of god, and he blesses us with his favor. And it is his will that we should..."

"You talk to god and he responds?" curiously interrupted the Duke.

"Why yes, my son. God hears our voices when we lift them up in prayer."

"Great, then maybe he can find you a new home," quipped the Duke, slamming the door in the old abbot's face.

CHAPTER 4: THE MODEL

Oleg stood alone in the cavernous room that had once been the monks' dining hall. Two rows of dining chairs stood stacked up in lines against the far wall on either side of the room's fireplace. They had been moved there sometime ago in order to better facilitate access to the massively long table which filled the room's center. Upon the table, there sat an elaborate scale model of the city of Siztok.

"Oh, Oleg," gasped out Oleg, poorly attempting to mimic the Duke.

In each hand he held a small crudely carved wooden figure. He had drawn a rough beard on one figure that approximated his own while on the other he had drawn a uniform that more or less represented Duke Belloch's.

"Oh, Oleg," repeated Oleg in mimic, lightly shaking the Duke figurine. "You're so strong and so manly, you should be the real king, and I should give you eighty wives."

"Oleg," whispered a voice directly behind him.

"AHHHHH!" screamed out Oleg in surprise, dropping the two figures upon the model city before him.

Both figures landed upon a paper building, crushing it. Instantly, Oleg spun in place, finding himself face to face with Duke Belloch.

"Are you breaking my new model?" asked Duke Belloch.

"No boss, no... I'm sorry."

"That's alright," reassured the Duke with uncharacteristic charity. "Just make sure you fix it."

"I didn't even hear you walk up, boss."

"It's my new slippers," bragged Belloch, pointing down at the fuzzy blue slippers which rested upon his feet. "I saw the cutest little lamb the other day, and thought 'Ohhhh, that creature would make the most comfortable slippers,' and guess what?"

"What?"

"I was right!" joyfully exclaimed the Duke. "It's like walking on clouds."

tap *tap* *tap* Both men turned as one towards the gentle tapping sound which emanated from the room's south door. There they saw a portly head, adorned by a golden chain which held the gold seal of the city upon it, peaking in.

"Good Lord Mayor!" declared the Duke, throwing his arms wide open.

"You called for me, M'Lord?" groveled the Mayor, stepping timidly into the room.

"I most certainly did. Come quick, come see my

newest model."

The Lord Mayor scurry-waddled across the former dining room until he too stood beside the large model of the city.

"Behold the future of Siztok," beamed Belloch, like a child showing off a new toy. "My architect has outdone himself. Look at the detail on the miniature buildings, exquisite. There, of course, is the capital building that we currently stand in and the surrounding uptown region. Notice that it is untouched, except for the fact that we have reinforced the inner wall which encircles uptown."

"Inner wall?" asked a confused Lord Mayor.

"Oleg," inquired the Duke. "How is the reinforcement of the inner wall going in real life?"

"Almost done boss. A couple more days maximum and it'll be finished."

"Excellent work!" declared the Duke, handing out some rare praise. "Now, Lord Mayor, everything beyond the inner wall is new. We're going to build a second wall, a greater one, that encircles the entire city. One so large and thick that a thousand sieges engines could not penetrate it."

Eagerly, Duke Belloch leaned over the model tracing the outline of the outer wall with his finger, then he began to point out regions within its confines.

"There, in the north of the city, we will build our immense textile houses and grand market places. We shall have a dozen gates in the north wall, allowing caravans from the northern plantations to send us their goods."

Quickly, Duke Belloch sidestepped to his left, pointing to the south end of the city model.

"And there, in the south, we shall build our great mills and silos. We shall have a dozen gates in the south wall, allowing caravans from the southern plantations to send us their produce. The great silos will hold enough food to last for years. And in the west wall, we shall build a great gate for our main road, Belloch's Highway. Along that major artery we shall send out our multitude of goods, far and wide, for sale, and they will bring back cartloads of gold."

While Duke Belloch smiled pridefully, a look of consternation began to creep upon the Lord Mayor's face.

"What about the poor?" cautiously asked the Lord Mayor, staring at the model city between the inner wall and the proposed outer wall.

"Oh, I can't stand them. Disgustingly ignorant things."

"Agreed," replied the Mayor. "But, on your model, the slums are gone... where will the poor live?"

"I don't caaaare," declared the Duke. "Just get rid of them. Well, except the ones we need to work the mills and textile houses."

The Lord Mayor paused for a moment, eyes fixed upon the model.

"Your Grace, even if I wanted too..." the Lord Mayor's words stopped dead in their tracks under Duke Belloch's harsh sidelong glare. "Err... I mean, I most certainly wish I could, but the city doesn't have enough guards to do that, and worse, if we tried and failed, we could have a full grown rebellion on our hands."

"Oleg?" said the Duke, looking toward the barbarian.

"I hate to agree with the esteemed Lord Mayor," spat out Oleg, glaring jealously at the Lord Mayor's golden seal. "Even with the army, killing and enslaving the whole poor quarters would be a dicey proposition. We have the training and discipline, but they way way out number us. Could go either way. It'd be easier if we had some act of god, like a fire or a flood to thin them out first."

"Gods forbid," shuddered the Lord Mayor, gripping the golden seal around his neck.

"Agreed," nodded the Duke with an approving grin towards Oleg. "The gods forbid indeed."

CHAPTER 5: HOLY MEN

As the rose colored skies of early twilight filled the heavens above, the long shadows of evening began to creep between the claustrophobically close decrepit wood shacks that filled Siztok's immense slums. And in their midst, along one the of the slums' many filth covered crooked roads, there stood a small circle of a dozen robed men.

"Brothers!" declared the elderly former abbot of St. Ufstath's cathedral. "Though our numbers have dwindled much in the weeks since our expulsion from our holy home, despite our hardships, we have found a new home here in the slums amongst the poor and the downtrodden. Those of you who still remain are the true servants and prophets of the Lord, for our Lord is not of earth, but of heaven."

"Amen," agreed the robed men as one.

"This is most certainly a sign from on high," instructed the abbot. "That from now on our duty is to attended to the needs of the poor. To comfort and aid them in their times of pain and sorrow. To be a guiding light of purity and goodness, steering them from the rocky shores of sin as St. Ufstath himself once did."

"Amen," agreed the robed men as one.

"Now let us go out, tending to the flock, helping the helpless."

"Amen," agreed the congregated robed men.

With a prideful smile, the elderly abbot watched his remaining holy order slowly disperse in their mission to help the poor. Then he too turned down a small alley in search of the same. He didn't have far to travel before his nose was offended by the sulfuric smell of rotten eggs. There, in a dark corner of the alley, was the source of the putrid emanation. A wild man, with a wild beard upon his face and a lit torch in one hand, who was busily rooting about in a nearby trashcan.

After saying a brief silent prayer for the wild man's soul, the elderly abbot kindly approached.

"Oh, brother," consoled the monk. "You look like you've fallen on hard times. Hard times come to us all, but our heavenly Lord will see us through with mercy, forgiveness, and grace... wait, wait! You're one of those donkey dicks that stole our home from us!"

CRAAACK The world went temporarily black for the abbot as Oleg's fist once again collided with the abbot's skull.

CHAPTER 6: THE BRIGADE

Dusk around him, torch in hand, Oleg rushed up the road towards the great gate that cut Siztok in two.

"Open the gate!" loudly commanded Oleg.

"Immediately, sir!" came the reply from the guard atop the wall.

Slowly, the great wooden doors swung open, revealing the opulence of the upper city. And there, just inside the upper city, stood Duke Belloch himself and a company of his finest men. Upon his figure, he wore an expertly tailored uniform of the fire brigade. Wasting no time, Oleg scurried toward the Duke.

"It's done, boss."

"Get rid of that thing, you imbecile," commanded Belloch through gritted teeth, glancing at the lit torch.

Oleg looked around for a moment, then tossed the flaming torch, quenching it in one of the many water filled fire brigade buckets that lined the street. As Oleg and the Duke conversed in hushed tones, a small group of rich Siztokians began to assemble, gawking at the unexpected sight of Belloch and his fire brigade.

"Your Lordship! Your Lordship!" came the familiar voice of the Lord Mayor, his body jiggling as he waddled over toward the men.

"What's going on?"

"A uncontrollable fire has broken out in the slums," explained the Duke. "It's been raging for half an hour."

"Fifteen minutes," corrected Oleg.

"Fifteen minutes?" erupted Duke Belloch, glaring at Oleg. "Cause it seems like it SHOULD have been half an hour."

The Lord Mayor never even saw Oleg shrug in response. In the fading lights of the gloaming, through the open gate, the Lord Mayor's eyes frantically scanned the massive dark slums below. At first he saw nothing, but then a distant dot of flames arose, and then another, then and another. Slowly, far off, a great wall of smoke began to climb into the air.

"Assemble the fire brigades!" cried out the Lord Mayor. "Hurry your Grace, we must put out the fires."

The Lord Mayor felt a calm gloved hand wrap around his shoulder.

"I'm afraid," fawned the Duke in false sincerity. "That it is much too late. The fire is much too extensive."

Duke Belloch took a step towards the growing assembly of the anxious rich.

"Fear not good people of the upper city!" cried out Belloch. "I, your Lord, have placed my fire

32

brigades along every gate. We shall fight these flames, tooth and nail. I shall be the guardian of both your health and your wealth."

A grateful cheer arose from the crowd.

"Help us!" cried out a pitiful woman's voice.

The crowd turned as one. There, on the poor side of the gate, they saw a woman in singed clothes, holding a young baby. Quickly, a new crowd was assembling around the poor woman. They wore clothes, both dirty and burnt, for they were the poor of Siztok's lower city. Though the gate that joined the upper and lower cities stood open, they dared not step into the home of the rich.

"Help us!" cried out the woman again, holding up her baby. "If not for me, then for my child."

"Shut the gate!" yelled out the Lord Mayor, rushing toward the gate.

"NO!" refuted the Duke. "Belay that order."

The guard atop the wall stood there confused, gazing down on the two groups below: the rich in the upper city, and the imperiled poor in the lower city.

"It's alright," assured Duke Belloch to all around. "Come in woman, come in, and bring your ugly baby with you. To the poor of Siztok! Come in, and bring all of your ugly babies with you! Together we shall take cover in the might of the upper city's walls, which, I might add, have been reinforced by myself, providing extra fire safety at no additional cost to yourselves. I, Duke Belloch the magnanimous, shall protect you all."

Oleg, the Lord Mayor, and the rich of Siztok warily eyed the stream of charred and soiled refugees that began to pour into the upper city.

"This wasn't my original plan," whispered Oleg in confidence to the Duke.

"No, no it's not," beamed Duke Belloch. "It's even better. Soon this fire will have cleared out those unsightly slums, making way for my new construction projects, AND, due to having saved their lives, we'll have a very motivated and loyal work force. LORD MAYOR!"

Angrily, the Lord Mayor stomped toward Duke Belloch.

"This, this, this is too much your Grace!" stammered the Lord Mayor. "We can't have the poor living up here, in the upper city!"

"Are you challenging me?" coldly inquired the Duke, staring into the Lord Mayor's eyes.

Awkwardly, the Lord Mayor glanced toward Oleg for help, but found none.

"Ummm, no your Grace. I just mean..."

"Have some faith in me," interrupted Duke Belloch. "I agree, in the long term, the poor can not stay here, BUT, in the meantime we will have to make due. Tomorrow, or the next day, when the fire is out, you will announce the "Homes for Work" program. The victims of this terrible fire shall not be forgotten by their generous lord."

"Who's that?" densely grunted Oleg.

"It's me you moron," snapped the Duke. "Now shut up. Where was I? Oh yes, those who are willing to work in cleaning the rubble, and in building the businesses of tomorrow, shall be granted a brand new home of their own when the construction is finished."

"Oh, that's excellent," smiled the Lord Mayor, clapping his hands in joy. "The best of a bad situation. You get your new textile houses, mills, and outer wall, and the poor get grand homes of their own."

"Suuuure," noncommittally replied the Duke. "Now do me a favor and go appease that group of rich residents. Let them know that the poor being here is just temporarily."

"Yes, your Grace."

"Oh, and Lord Mayor."

"Yes?"

"Do it quickly," sighed the Duke. "I fear that Lady Victoria is trying to make eyes at me again."

"Immediately, M'Lord," bowed the Lord

Mayor, before rushing off.

But all that was many months ago.

CHAPTER 7: CHAINED

The song of the tired and weary, the shackled and enslaved, drifted forlornly across the plains. The song sang not of justice, for there was none here. It sang not of hope, for that had died long ago.

Bound by cold iron chains; hundreds of men, women, and children toiled away in the plantation's great northern wheat field. Their skin was browned and burned by the Steppe's harsh sun. Some wore weathered horse leather jerkins upon their bodies that hinted back to better days. Some wore nothing all. Yet all labored under the crack of the whip and the watchful eyes of the assembled guards.

CRAAACK

"OWWW!" painfully cried out a small child, feeling the cut of the whip bite into her unprotected flesh.

"Back to work," commanded a guard with a cruel smile.

The guard, like the couple dozen who patrolled the northern wheat field, wore a pristine purple uniform and sat upon brown horse. He carried a sword on one hip and a whip on the other. Lazily, he lifted a canteen to his lips, taking a great drink as several thirsty slaves jealously watched on.

The Westernson plantation was an odd sight.

Located less than a day's march south by south west from Siztok, it stood out like a sore thumb in the wild flatlands of the Steppes of Rannsaka. Excepting a small forest which straddled a little river that ran along the plantation's northwest border, the vast plantation grounds were encircled by an ocean of prairie grass that spread to the horizon in all directions.

In the center of the grounds, surrounded by massive wheat fields on all sides, there stood a grand plantation house. Dominatingly, it towered over all like a great white temple dedicated to Duke Belloch's greed. On sunny days, its gleaming white colonnades, which held up the palatial house's great roof and supported its wide balcony porches, could be seen from miles away. Across a field of waist high wheat, built at an angle so as not to be seen from the plantation house's grand porch, there lay a row of long, squat, dilapidated slave quarters.

If any of the guards had bothered to turn southwest at that moment, they might have seen a metallic glint of light which shone in the distance.

On the plantation's far edge, where the prairie grass met the cultivated fields, Pavel hid. The former barbarian wore faded brown trousers upon his legs and a food soiled white shirt upon his torso. Cautiously, he steadied his trusty old bronze spyglass against his right eye, surveying the plantation ahead.

"Well?" asked a familiar voice from behind him. "Are they there?"

Pavel lowered the spyglass from his eye and turned toward the sound of the voice. There, crouched in the tall grass, was his chief and friend, Menderchuck. Menderchuck wore a rough cut horse leather jerkin upon his body, and upon his belt there hung a white bone handle knife and a great curved saber. The wild beard, which covered Menderchuck's face, did little to conceal his concern.

"I don't know," admitted Pavel with a tinge of defeat in his voice. "Maybe we should find another plantation. The slaves, they're definitely from the horse clans, but I don't see anyone that I recognize. Our people might not be here."

"Well," declared Menderchuck. "We can work ·with that."

"Can we?" doubtfully asked Torfulson.

Menderchuck turned to look towards his son. Slightly taller than his father and clean shaven, Torfulson wore the clothes of an Oppidian peasant upon his body. Nervously, he patted the side of his donkey Muffin, who was eagerly enjoying a feast of the bountiful grass which filled the wide open plains.

"Of course we can," reassured Menderchuck. "I am the chief of the great clan Chuck."

"Was the leader," corrected Pavel.

"There's still three of us, it's still a thing," plowed on Menderchuck, undeterred. "We are the last unconquered clan... even if we did get conquered, but that was before Torf joined. Clan Chuck is back, and we're better than ever, baby!"

Torfulson cast an uncertain glance upon his father.

Like sudden storm clouds passing before the sun, so too did Menderchuck's countenance darken. Even after all this time, he could still hear their cries. He could still see their dead and mutilated bodies. Those he had called friend, family, and clan brother. All wiped out long ago by Belloch's marauding army.

"If even a single one of our people still live," grimly announced Menderchuck. "We owe it to them to rescue them from Belloch's evil clutches. And these other folks, these slaves, like us, were once horse riders. Whether ours or not, they need our help. No man should be a slave. I am the last free chief of the plains. Don't you think that it makes sense for them to follow me in rebellion?"

"I do," skeptically answered Pavel. "But I'm not so sure they'll feel the same way."

"Of course they will," grinned Menderchuck, his countenance lighting. "Now, what are we up against?"

"There's a lot of guards. And they are heavily armed. They might be Butarian mercenaries."

"How many, exactly?" asked Menderchuck.

Peeking his head just above the grass line, Pavel turned back towards the plantation. Once again he lifted his bronze spyglass to his eye. Studiously, he surveyed the extensive plantation for several silent minutes.

"40, maybe 43 guards," doubtfully ventured Pavel. "At least that I can see."

Torfulson's heart sunk at Pavel's words. There were only three of them and at least forty guards to deal with. Menderchuck shifted his legs, resting his hand on the hilt of his legendary sword Arbjak as the gears inside of his head began to grind.

"Well, on a good day, I could take on maybe ten of them at once," ventured Menderchuck.

"I could fight five," added Pavel.

Menderchuck gave Pavel a seriously annoyed look.

"If I'm lucky, maybe six."

Menderchuck nodded, that was a much better number. Then there was silence. Menderchuck and Pavel glanced expectantly at Torfulson, who was absentmindedly staring at the distant palatial plantation house.

"What?" asked Torfulson finally taking notice of both men's gaze.

"How many could you fight?" inquired Menderchuck.

"Zero," replied Torfulson.

"Zero?!!!" erupted Menderchuck.

"Shhhh, we don't want to be discovered!" hushed Pavel, desperately trying to calm Menderchuck, but it was to no avail.

"Zero?!?!?" Menderchuck ranted at his son. "You single handedly defeated the great mother beast of the Chilopo, and you're telling me you can't slay a single guard?!"

"I had no choice! The creature swallowed me whole," replied an indignant Torfulson. "What do you want me to do?! Dress up as a turkey dinner and hope these guards swallow me whole?!"

Menderchuck suddenly became still. His eyes drifted up towards the sky, glazing over. Pavel had seen this look many times before. Usually it meant that Menderchuck was about to say something really stupid.

"No," preempted Pavel.

"What? I haven't even said anything yet!"

"No," repeated Pavel.

Excitedly, Menderchuck began to explain his new plan anyways.

"Just follow me. First we need to find a master cook, wait! Pavel, you're a master cook! You need to make the most delicious turkey dinner ever. It'll smell so good that they'll just swallow it whole."

"No," stoically repeated Pavel.

"A turkey is too big to swallow whole," added a confused Torfulson.

"Fine, something smaller, like a squab," eagerly continued Menderchuck. "Thennnnnnn, we find a wizard, and get them to shrink us down to the size of a mouse or something, then we can hide in the food. The food'll smell so good that they swallow us whole. They'll all be like, 'What a great meal, I swallow it so fast it was so good. Now to lay with my ugly wife, aggghh, akkkkk, splat.' Our tiny blades will stab out of them, and blood flows everywhere, as tiny us emerges victoriously."

"No," repeated Pavel again.

"Are there even any wizards around here?" inquired Torfulson.

Torfulson had a point. Wizards were a rare sight in this part of the world.

"Fine," whined Menderchuck. "If you're so smart, than how are we going to free these people?"

Torfulson turned towards Pavel, "May I borrow your spyglass, please?"

With a friendly nod, Pavel placed his spyglass into Torfulson's hand. Torfulson then lifted the spyglass to his eye and took his turn surveying the plantation grounds.

"Well," began Torfulson, his eye still on the spyglass. "The guards are heavily armed, but they aren't wearing much in the way of armor. They've just got uniforms on. We should sneak up and stealth kill three of them. Then we disguise ourselves in their uniforms and infiltrate the camp as guards."

"I'm in," agreed Pavel.

"Not as good as my turkey dinner plan," sulked Menderchuck. "But I guess we can try it YOUR way."

CHAPTER 8: TORFULSON'S PLAN

The guard's eyelids drooped for a moment, lulled to rest by the calm rhythmic sounds of the warm afternoon wind pushing the wheat stalks in waves around him. Dressed in a clean white shirt and purple uniform trousers lined with silver piping, he took half a step back, rested his hand upon his sword's hilt, and surveyed the great western wheat field around him.

"Bill island," thought the guard to himself, as though he were the lone island in a great sea of wheat.

Little did he know that he wasn't alone. Hidden below the surface of the rolling wheat, only twenty feet behind him, were three men. Sweaty and tired, it had taken the three men the better part of an hour, crawling upon their bellies, to sneak up upon the guard undetected. Now though, they had reached a crossroads of indecision.

"So far so good. I don't think he's seen us," conspiratorially whispered Torfulson while Pavel watched on for guidance. "Do you think it'd be better if we sneak up the rest of the way on our bellies, or should we split up and..."

"Hey, there's a delicious turkey dinner over here!" shouted out Menderchuck, who was still hidden in the wheat.

Instantly, fear leapt up into Torfulson's throat

while his eyes filled with surprise.

"What are you doing?!" furiously whispered Torfulson.

Menderchuck merely pointed up through the wheat toward the armed guard. The guard turned around and raised a hand to his eyes, shielding them from the afternoon sun. For a moment, he looked over the immense wheat field, seeing nothing. Then he reached down, pulled his short sword from his scabbard, and began to advance menacingly forward.

"See!" triumphantly whispered Menderchuck. "I told you that the turkey dinner plan would have worked. Look how quickly he's coming this way. Everyone likes turkey!"

"He must have excellent hearing. He's headed straight towards us," whispered a growingly concerned Pavel.

"And he's got a sword," added an anxious Torfulson, who had just become acutely aware of the fact that he had no weapon himself.

crunch *crunch* *crunch* Trampled wheat stalks in his wake, step by step, the armed guard approached the three men's hiding place.

"Maybe we should rush him," urgently whispered Torfulson.

crunch *crunch* *crunch*

"We should jump him, like now! Right guys?...

guys?" Torfulson's whispered pleas were once again met with silence.

crunch *crunch* *crunch*

Frantically, Torfulson's head spun to the left to confer with Menderchuck and Pavel, but to his dismay he saw no one there. Desperately, Torfulson's head twisted to the right, looking in vain for his allies, but to his horror he once again saw no one there.

"Surrender and die!" shouted the guard.

Fear gripping his soul, Torfulson slowly turned his head toward the sound, finding the guard's blade only inches from his face.

"Sh.. Sh… Shouldn't it be surrender or die?" weakly sputtered Torfulson, anxiously looking up at the guard.

The guard spat down on Torfulson.

"Get up slave, or I'll make a eunuch of you!"

Defensively covering his crotchular region, Torfulson slowly rose to his feet, eyes darting about in search of his father and Pavel. For the briefest of moments, his anger at having been abandoned overwhelmed his fear of being castrated.

"Those sons of a poohead!" angrily spat out Torfulson under his breath.

"What did you call me?" wondered the guard.

"Nothing, sir," gulped Torfulson.

"ATTACK!!!" rang out Menderchuck's voice as he suddenly appeared from the wheat, throwing dirt into the guard's eyes.

"AHHHHH!!!!" screeched the guard, grasping his face in pain and dropping his sword to the ground.

The clamorous sounds of Menderchuck's battle cry and the guard's screech raced each other across the fields toward the distant plantation house. In a short moment, a new sound joined their chorus of cacophony, the plantation's alarm bell.

"ATTTACK!!!" screamed out Pavel, emerging from the wheat, gripping the guard's arms from behind, and pinning them tight.

"Uuhh, Good I guess," stammered the confused Torfulson. "Get his uniform...

Torfulson's words were too late. Menderchuck had already pulled his white bone handle knife from his belt, leapt toward the restrained guard, and begun stabbing him wildly like a pincushion.

The knife's blade flashed in the afternoon sun as it quickly, repeatedly, brutally pierced the guard's body. Each steely knife bite tore a new blood soaked hole in the guard's formerly white shirt. Body slumping, blood gushing, the final drops of life drained from his body. Pavel then released the guard's lifeless corpse which collapsed to the ground.

"Success!" declared Menderchuck, beaming victoriously.

"Huzzah!" joyously cried out Pavel.

Torfulson, face full of anguish and frustration, glared at his two compatriots.

"What are you doing?!" shouted Torfulson.

"Your plan," sincerely answered Menderchuck. "We're supposed to kill a guard. Did you forget your plan? It's ok, I forget things too at times."

"NO!" shouted Torfulson. "I didn't forget my plan! My plan was to stealth kill three guards and steal their uniforms. Does it look like we can use his uniform?!"

Torfulson pointed down at the dead guard. The guard's trousers and torn white shirt were drenched in blood.

"You weren't supposed to stab him!" furiously cried out Torfulson.

"How else was I going to kill him?" asked Menderchuck.

"I don't know, smother him, crush his wind pipe. Anything, so that we could use the uniform as a disguise! That was the plan we agreed to!"

"You agreed to it!" argued Menderchuck. "I wanted to do the turkey dinner plan!"

"Put the clothes on! Put the clothes on!" commanded Pavel's suddenly frantic voice.

As one, Torfulson and Menderchuck looked toward Pavel, then followed his fear filled eyes towards the great plantation house. To their dismay, a new guard was rapidly approaching their position. And to their even greater dismay, a great company of distant guards were in fast pursuit.

"GLENN!" cried out the rapidly approaching lead guard. "I might have some runaways!"

Instantly, Menderchuck and Pavel dropped down, disappearing into the waist high wheat. For the briefest of moments, Torfulson froze. Then he felt a hand reach up out of the wheat, roughly grab his shirt, quickly pulling him out of sight, down into the wheat.

"Identify yourself," called out the guard in a firm voice, unleashing his sword from its scabbard. "Surrender now!"

The gentle sounds of the wind pushing through the stalks of wheat was the only response. Briefly, the guard paused, staring up at the spot where the three men had disappeared. Then, boots crushing the wheat stalks before him, the guard began to boldly advance in their direction.

crunch *crunch* *crunch*

"Identify yourself," commanded the guard again. "Surrender now, and we may let you live."

crunch *crunch* *crunch*

"Hi," awkwardly greeted Torfulson, his voice cracking as he suddenly popped up out of the wheat field before the guard.

Startled, the guard took half a step backwards, eyes transfixed upon the horrid sight before him. Clinging to his body like rain drenched clothing, Torfulson wore the dead guard's blood soaked torn shirt upon his torso, and upon his legs he wore the dead guard's blood stained trousers.

"Oh my gods, are you alright?" gasped out the lead guard, fearing that one of his own had been injured.

"Yeah... ummmm, yeah, I'm fine," squeaked Torfulson. "Ummm, you know, just doing guard things... that we do."

"What?" asked the confused guard.

"Errr, catching some escaped slaves and all that," scrambled Torfulson, his mind racing. "Oh, look, I.. I... I have got them here."

While Torfulson fearfully looked past the guard toward the distant company of guards that were rapidly approaching, the lone guard looked confusedly at the empty wheat field around them.

"I said!" repeated Torfulson in a louder voice, his arms gesturing wildly. "I have the escaped slaves right here!"

Pavel, crouched down upon his knees in hiding, suddenly realized what Torfulson was alluding to. Grabbing Menderchuck by the arm, Pavel rose to his feet, pulling his chief up with him.

"Oh drat, you got us," awkwardly stated Pavel. "I guess it's back to slavery for us."

"You're going to be whipped to an inch of your life for such an act!" threatened the guard, waving his sword.

"No, oh, no," worriedly interjected Torfulson. "I mean, maybe this time, we should just let them off with a warning... or something. And then next time, if they do it again, then we do the whipping thing."

The guard's eyes narrowed, skeptically judging Torfulson.

"Now you slaves," stiltedly lectured Torfulson. "Don't you go about trying to escape again."

"Never sir, we've learned our lesson," obediently replied Pavel.

Menderchuck stood there sulkily, until Pavel jabbed him in the ribs with his elbow.

"What he said!" agreed Menderchuck.

While the perplexed guard stood there actively trying to process it all, a particularly strong gust of wind pushed through the wheat revealing the dead guard's naked corpse.

"And who's that?!" gasped out the lead guard, pointing his sword towards the deceased.

"Uhhh, uhhhh," stumbled Torfulson. "An escaped slave. He stabbed me, so I had to kill him."

With a furrowed brow, the guard studied the bloody torn shirt upon Torfulson's body.

"Waaait," began the guard. "Your shirt is all cut and bloody, but your chest doesn't have any cuts."

"Like I said, he stabbed my shirt. So I had to kill him."

"That's what I saw," added Menderchuck. "As a slave, which I am, I'm all for escaping, but killing guards is wrong."

A very quizzical look worked its way upon the guard's face. For a moment he stared over at Menderchuck, then looked down to the corpse, then back up to Menderchuck, and finally back down to the corpse.

"That's a lot of blood," grimaced the guard. "But that, that slave's face... you're sure he's a slave?"

"Yup," replied all three men in suspicious unison.

"Well..." continued the guard, tilting his head as he looked down upon the corpse. "The dead slave's face looks a bit like that other guard... what's his name?... Bill. Don't ya think?"

Pavel wasted no time.

"Look at me! Look at me! I'm escaping again! I just can't help myself!"

Spinning on his heels as he shouted, Pavel darted out of reach of the lurching guard, running off into the field. The moment that the guard was distracted, Menderchuck desperately scanned the ground. Not far away, there lay a large field stone. Menderchuck scurried toward it, straining for a moment, lifting it with both hands, then rushed back with it towards the corpse.

CRACK

With a mighty hurl, Menderchuck brought the large stone crashing down upon the dead guard's head. Like a sledgehammer meeting a watermelon, the corpse's skull shattered with a loud crack and a wet squish.

"What in the world was that?" blurted out the lead guard, turning from the escaping Pavel toward the dead guard's corpse.

"I didn't hear anything," ventured Torfulson.

"Me either," added Menderchuck.

The guard looked down at the shattered bone, squished flesh, and brains that had once been the corpse's head.

"Hey wait, what happened to that dead guy's face?" curiously asked the guard.

"Nothing," quickly replied Torfulson.

"What? He was already like that," added Menderchuck.

As the last word slipped from Menderchuck's mouth, the great company of guards, who had rushed across the wheat field, finally arrived.

"Glenn," commanded the lead guard. "I'm going..."

"Oh, I'm going to enjoy so much freedom!" yelled out Pavel, taunting the guards from the field's far edge. "Eat my buttocks, you smelly guards!"

"No one calls me smelly!" erupted the lead guard, furious at Pavel's antics. "Glenn, take these two! Bring the slave to the pit, and bring the guard to the foreman."

"But... but..." sputtered Glenn.

"Do it now!" shouted the lead guard, before gesturing to the troop. "And the rest of you! Follow me! Five gold pieces to the one that brings me that slave's head!"

Glenn pouted as the other guards cheered, running off across the field in hot pursuit of Pavel.

CHAPTER 9: THE PRISONER

"Hurry up," roughly commanded Glenn, shoving the barbarian from behind.

With a grunt, Menderchuck stumbled awkwardly forward. As he regained his balance, he shot a furious yet brief glare back in Glenn's direction. Together, the three men (Torfulson the fake guard, Glenn the real guard, and Menderchuck the prisoner) marched eastward through the wheat field toward the great plantation house.

"Sooo," asked Glenn, gesturing toward Torfulson's torn and bloody garment. "What in the world happened to your shirt?"

"Killed a slave," lied Torfulson.

"Oh, that's awesome," smiled Glenn. "Good job! You new here?"

"Ummm, yeahhhh. I... I'm Torfulson."

"I thought so," eagerly clapped Glenn. "Well, I mean, I didn't know that was your name, but I could tell you were new. I didn't recognize your face. Oh, I'm Glenn, by the way. I know most everyone here by now, but that changes every week."

"How so?"

"We get new guards in here all the time," explained Glenn. "The foreman scares a number of them off. He's a bit of a jerk. His bark is worse than his bite though... well, ummmm, unless he turns his whip or sword on you, then maybe his bite is worse. He's an expert with that whip. One time he bet us that he could whip the fly straight off of a slave's face. And you know what?!"

"No," mumbled Torfulson, not quite sure as to where Glenn's story was going.

"He did it!" energetically erupted Glenn. "I mean, sure, he took the slave's eye out, but he technically got the fly too. I won two whole guilders on that bet! You could say that it was a pretty lucky day."

"Probably not for the slave."

"Ehhhh," shrugged Glenn. "His fault, he should have kept an eye out for it. Ha ha ha!"

Glenn burst out in robust laughter at his own joke as his two traveling companions exchanged sidelong glances.

"You know," bragged Glenn. "I'm kinda the funny guy on this plantation. Now, what was I saying? Oh yeah, we get a lot of new guards here. It's tough work and often the new guards just don't have the stomach for it. Folks will line up for a paycheck, but the moment you gotta cripple a runaway, well, a lot of new guys balk at that."

Glenn took a second look at Torfulson's bloody shirt before continuing, "But I'm guessing that's not going to be a problem for you."

"No! No! No!" suddenly gasped out Torfulson like a parent trying to stop a young child from doing something disastrous.

Torfulson darted out in front of Menderchuck, gripping the barbarian's wrist. It was then that Glenn noticed Menderchuck's hand reaching toward the white bone handle knife that hung upon his belt.

"Hey, you're not supposed to have those!" fearfully screamed out Glenn, leaping backward, awkwardly fumbling for his own sword.

"It's ok, it's ok," assured Torfulson, carefully pulling the knife and sword from Menderchuck's belt. "Those are mine, I was just having him hold them for me while I crushed the other slave with a rock."

Glenn's brows furrowed, skeptically judging Torfulson.

"I don't know," grimly began Glenn. "Either you're the dumbest guard I ever met or a liar."

The air in the wheat field hung particularly heavy over the three men as each stood resolute in a silent stand off.

"Uhhhhh," stumbled Torfulson. "Is it just me... or is the tension getting thick... so thick, you could almost cut it with a knife."

Torfulson smiled weakly as he awkwardly pantomimed cutting the air with the white bone handle knife.

"Ha, ha, ha!" roared Glenn with laughter. "That's a good one. That's a good one. I better watch out for you. I might have a challenger for funniest guard."

Torfulson's whole body deflated like a worn out balloon, letting out a long sigh of relief.

"Oh, that's a nice sword," added Glenn, pointing towards Menderchuck's saber. "Can I hold it?"

"Absolutely not," Menderchuck grumpily scoffed.

"Shut up slave," commanded Torfulson, handing the legendary blade Arbjak to Glenn the guard.

Hilt in hand, Glenn the guard studied the blade, bouncing it slightly in his grip.

"It's got good balance," admired Glenn.

Suddenly Glenn swung the sword above his head in a wild arc, stopping just short of Torfulson.

"Surrender," grimly commanded Glenn, holding the blade menacingly toward Torfulson.

"Uhhh... ok," sputtered Torfulson, lifting his hands.

"I get what's going on now," coolly drawled Glenn. "This sword is amazing! No wonder you had him hold it for you. I wouldn't want it to get rusty on the ground either. You're so lucky. I wish this was mine. Just a word of advice though, don't ever let the foreman see it in a slave's hands, or he'll most likely fire you."

In one swift move, Glenn flipped the saber, offering it hilt first back to Torfulson.

"Thanks, I'll remember that..." gasped Torfulson, recovering Arbjak.

"Come on, let's go," encouraged a smiling Glenn.

With Glenn in the lead, the three men resumed their journey toward the great plantation house. In short order, he had lead them out of the western fields and into the sunny side of the great plantation house. As they approached the great white walled house, Glenn slowed, allowing Menderchuck and Torfulson to pass him. To Torfulson's surprise, he felt Glenn's hand upon his shoulder, bringing him to a halt. Obliviously, Menderchuck took several steps more, then suddenly collapsed.

donnnng Rung out the hard sound of Menderchuck's falling body colliding with metal.

"huuuuuuuuuu!" squeaked out Menderchuck's pained cry, desperately sucking in air.

"Ha, ha, ha, ha!" bellowed out Glenn's joyous

laughter.

Hastily, Torfulson leapt forward to check on his father. To his great surprise, he discovered Menderchuck shaking in pain, grasping his groin, his legs draped through the top bars of a cruel cage.

The cage was submerged in a square hole that was ten feet wide, ten feet long, and twelve feet deep. The top of the metal cage was flush with the surrounding ground. Its bars were worn and weathered and its floor was covered in puddles of mud and human feces. Torfulson glanced down apprehensively at the submerge cage and smelled the faint acrid scent of death.

"You gotta be careful," spouted Glenn between laughs. "It's hard to see the pit until you come up to it. Last week a horse escaped and broke its legs on it."

Torfulson put a wary leg upon one of the cage's top bars and bent down. Then he steadied Menderchuck, helping him free his legs from the cage. Together, they pushed back onto the firm grass, looking down into the forlorn pit.

"Awww, crap," pouted Glenn. "We gotta get the key. Do you know where it is?"

Torfulson shook his head no.

"That's fine, that's fine," assured Glenn. "Just wait here with the slave. I'll be back."

Glenn bounced towards the great plantation

house, disappearing into the south servants' door. The moment that Glenn disappeared from sight, Torfulson spun toward his father.

"You don't have to do this," frantically whispered Torfulson. "This wasn't our plan, just run."

"No," stoically replied Menderchuck, glancing towards a group of distant slaves. "I won't abandon them."

"Do it, run! Get out of here," pleaded Torfulson. "I can still imitate a guard. I'll just say you overwhelmed me and escaped."

"No."

"I... I don't want to see you die, father," Torfulson's words faltered in his mouth.

"Then don't look," grinned Menderchuck.

"Ugh! I hate you," sulked Torfulson, rubbing his frustrated hands upon his own face.

"Hey, I found it!" interrupted Glenn's voice, shouting as he exited the plantation house, holding the key above him.

Glenn bounced back towards the pit, bending down besides the cage's metal gate. With a metallic click, his key unlocked the cage's rusty lock. The pit's metal gate creaked heavily as Glenn jerked it open. Then he stood upright, roughly grasped Menderchuck's arm, and began pushing him toward the pit's open gate.

"Ummm, let's lower him down," suggested Torfulson, grabbing Menderchuck's other arm.

"Usually the boys like to just push them down," replied Glenn. "Sometimes the slaves make a funny crunch sound when they hit bottom."

"Let's just lower him down," insisted Torfulson in a kind, but firm voice.

"You definitely are new here," smiled Glenn. "Where are you from?"

"I'm from Oppidium, maybe you heard of it?"

"No," answered Glenn. "Is it in on the plains? I'm from out west, near..."

"Can we get this butt sucking session over, and just drop me in the pit already?" interrupted Menderchuck. "You all are making me sick."

Torfulson and Glenn exchanged a glance, shrugged their shoulders, then carefully lowered Menderchuck down into the caged pit. Even so, the barbarian's feet couldn't reach bottom, and they had to drop him the last few feet. With a splash and a squish, Menderchuck landed deftly on his feet in the muddy prison below. At least he hoped that it was mud. Then he sat down.

As Torfulson wiped the sweat from his brow, Glenn slammed shut the cage's iron bar door, locking it tight.

"Sometimes at night," Glenn began. "Some of the boys will come out here and pee on the bars into the pit. Then they'll tell the slave inside that it's raining. It's kinda funny. It's a thing we do around here. You gotta have a sense of humor in this line of work. One time, this slave tried to drink it. I laughed so hard."

Torfulson winced at Glenn's story, but Glenn never noticed.

"Alright," declared Glenn, wiping the dust from his trousers. "Let's go find the foreman."

CHAPTER 10:
THE PLANTATION HOUSE

Like a dandelion seed floating upon a gentle summer's breeze, the plantation house's grand glass double doors glided open, revealing its palatial foyer. Copious amounts of light poured into room through a series of fifteen foot tall windows, brightly bouncing off of the room's elegant polished marble floor and its pristine white walls. Though the center of the foyer was empty to allow easy travel throughout the house, the edges of the room were decorated with expensive couches, elaborate gold statues, and, affixed to the walls, a multitude of fine paintings that were housed in golden frames.

As the two men entered the foyer, their foot steeps echoed out in the cavernous room. Astonished, Torfulson gazed up toward the enormous ceiling. There, his eyes beheld an immense golden chandelier. Above the chandelier, painted upon the ceiling itself, was a grand fresco of Duke Belloch leading his army to victory over the horse clans.

"Wow," awed Torfulson, beholding the opulence around him. "This is almost as grand as Visini's Opera House back home."

Closing the glass front doors behind them, Glenn pointed toward an elaborate embroidered couch which lay nearby.

"Wait here," instructed Glenn, glancing at Torfulson's bloody and torn guard uniform.

"Don't touch anything. Don't sit on anything. Ummm, just don't get blood on anything. I'll be back in a second. I gotta put the key away, then we'll go find the foreman."

Torfulson nodded timidly while Glenn marched across the white marble floor, disappearing through one of the many doors which lined the room. Torfulson's eyes then fell upon the monumental staircase which dominated the room's opposite end. Wide marble stairs, flanked by great banisters made of bronze and stone, led up to a second floor.

"Wow," whispered Torfulson to himself. "You could march a whole army up those stairs at the same time."

"Why can't you imbeciles take care of anything yourselves?!" screamed out a furious voice from atop the second floor, startling Torfulson.

It was then that the voice's owner stepped into view. Cresting the top of the staircase, was a tall intimidating man who was built like a brick house. The veins on his neck bulged with rage. He wore jet black riding pants upon his legs and well shined riding boots upon his legs. An ivory handle sword rested in a scabbard along his left hip, and a leather whip rested along his right. Six armed guards, dressed in crisp purple uniforms, followed closely behind him.

"Shake a leg, you lazy morons!" fiercely commanded the tall man.

Standing in front the luxurious couch beside the

glass double doors, Torfulson froze like a startled deer while the tall man and his guards rushed down the stairs straight towards him. The thunderous stomping of boots on marble echoed out ominously through the grand foyer as the group dismounted the stairs and sped across the floor, passing Torfulson without notice, pausing only for a moment to throw the front doors wide open.

Suddenly, the tall man stopped short. His guards desperately skidding to a halt behind him. Slowly, the tall man turned his head toward Torfulson.

The tall man stared for a moment, then blurted out, "What in the hells happened to you?!"

A tidal wave of panic washed over Torfulson. It screamed at him that the guards knew who he really was. It bellowed at him that the tall man was just toying with him. A jittering cold anxiety demanded that he run. That old familiar companion, doubt, warned him that he was too stupid to deceive the guards before him. In the midst of the emotional typhoon, a small ray of hope shown through. In that moment, he remembered the words of his father.

"The key to doing something illegal, is to act like you're supposed to be doing it," Menderchuck had instructed long ago. "Stay calm, act normal. If you do that, no one will ever question you."

"Killed a slave, sir," gulped Torfulson while seven pairs of eyes stared back at him.

The tall man rested his hand upon his sword's ivory hilt for a moment, judging Torfulson.

"One of the runaways?"

Torfulson said not a word, but slowly nodded his head.

"Good, good man," commended the tall man.

Then the tall man quickly turned to face the open door way, rapidly stepping toward it. As he began to leave, Torfulson let out a small sigh of relief.

"Foreman Collins! Foreman Collins!" shouted out Glenn, bursting into the room.

Torfulson's eyes went wide in fear.

"Not now Glenn!" snapped the tall man. "We have an emergency."

"Captain Lewis told me to bring the new guy to see you," declared Glenn, rushing across the marble floor, pointing a finger toward Torfulson.

"I've already seen him," curtly replied foreman Collins, turning back toward the wide open doorway.

Torfulson let out a second relieved sigh while foreman Collins and his entourage stepped out of the doorway.

"Wait!" cried out Glenn. "What do we do?"

Torfulson's body tightened as foreman Collins burst back into the grand foyer. For a moment the foreman stared at Torfulson, then he turned to glare at Glenn.

"Must I do everything myself?! Clean him up and get him a new uniform," angrily commanded the foreman. "Then get out to the north fields and help with guard duty. Don't let anymore of those animals escape."

"Yes, sir!" eagerly acknowledged Glenn.

Foreman Collins took two rushed steps towards the doorway, then stopped fast.

"Oh, and Glenn, don't take any of the horses. We need those for the search."

"Yes, sir," mumbled Glenn.

And with that, foreman Collins rushed out of the grand foyer, entourage in tow, slamming the double doors behind them.

"Well this is stupid," grumbled Glenn, sidling up to Torfulson. "Ughh... we're going to have to walk all the way out to the north field. Follow me, I'll show you where the spare uniforms are."

CHAPTER 11: THE PIT

If Duke Belloch had known that Menderchuck was currently alive and imprisoned at one of his many slave plantations, then things may have turned out very differently.

"Ugggh," weakly groaned Menderchuck, sitting alone in the thick mud.

Four days, for four days the defiant barbarian had wallowed in the rancid mud which covered the caged pit's floor. For four days, he had glanced forlornly at the dirt walls which surround the cage's cruel bars on all sides. For four days, he had stared up through the iron bars at the bright blue sky above, praying for freedom.

By day, the hot rays of the Steppes' harsh sun had beaten down into the pit, burning his skin. By night, the cold air of the Steppes' clear star filled night skies had poured down into the pit, chilling him to the bone.

"Water..." thirstily mumbled Menderchuck's parched lips as he stared at the muddy pools of water which surrounded him.

Well, at least he wished that it was water. The guards had a cruel habit of peeing down through the bars.

"Water!" they'd call out, before unleashing a stream.

Already three times today, he'd had to leap out of the way of the idiot guards who had stood above. Each guard laughing just a bit too hard at their own stupid joke. Menderchuck had to give them a bit of credit though. What they lacked in originality, they more than made up for with stubborn cruelty.

"Uh! What?!" flinched Menderchuck, hearing a sound above him.

As his eyes turned upward, he witnessed a plump crow fluttering down, landing on the bars high above. Menderchuck's starving stomach grumbled, and his mouth watered at such a tempting sight.

Cautiously, quietly, Menderchuck crept up to his feet, trying not to spook the bird. Gingerly, he arched his legs like a tiger preparing to pounce. Then he leapt up with all his might.

His outstretched fingers never even reached the top of the cage. As his body fell back towards the caged pit's floor, his feet hit its muddy surface and slipped.

"NOOO!" cried out Menderchuck, toppling face first into the muddy floor below.

SPLASH!

Hastily, Menderchuck, whose face and beard were drench in mud, pushed himself back up to his knees.

"Ewwww, gross!" sputtered Menderchuck,

spitting out a mouthful of rancid mud water.

Helplessly, he looked up toward bars above. Crestfallen, he watched the plump crow leap up into the air, flying off into the great blue sky.

CHAPTER 12: ST. UFSTATH'S

St. Ufstath's cathedral towered intimidatingly over the mansions of Siztok's rich. Its exquisite golden steeples had been torn down, replaced with new copper roofs that shone for miles around. The gold of the steeples had been melted down into statues and busts which glorified the likeness of Duke Belloch.

The massive ornate stained glass window of revered saints, that had stood in the cathedral's front wall for centuries, had been smashed to pieces. Now, in its place, there stood a majestic five story high marble balcony which looked out over the city.

A row of glass doors connected the elegant balcony's entrance to a great hall. In the before times, the great hall had been St Ufstath's 'shrine to all saints.' A cavernous collection of holy relics, masterful paintings, and elegant effigies dedicated to a plethora of pious people. A sort of "one stop shopping" experience for all that was good and holy.

The shrine had changed much since Duke Belloch's conquest. The holy relics and paintings had been smashed and burned as kindling. The effigies had been melted down for their precious metals. And in their places, there now stood honored relics of a new kind. Swords, shields, armor, and war banners (trophies of the Duke's conquests) now decorated the walls between new majestic paintings and golden busts that honored Duke Belloch.

"En garde," coolly declared Duke Belloch, his voice echoing out in the cavernous hall.

Two men stood in the center of the immense hall, swords in hands, facing each other. Compared to the enormity of the great hall, they looked quite small. A third portly man watched on with eager eyes.

Sword in hand, Oleg glanced across the massive hall at a large painting which dominated the room's west wall. It depicted the battle of Clan Chuck. A large hill occupied the right most of the landscape, and upon it, there stood the majestic archers of Duke Belloch. They poured their arrows into an army of horse raiders below.

The soldiers were painted as strong and clean. Whereas the horse raiders were painted with rotten teeth, scrawny arms, and evil glaring eyes. A single god ray poured down from the heavens and shone upon a mighty warrior who stood upon the archers' hill. It was the painted image of Duke Belloch himself. He stood defiantly with his sword raised high, directing the archers in their attack.

"Ughhhh," grunted Oleg, furrowing his eyebrows. "What's with the painting? You weren't even on the archers' hill during the battle. That should be me."

Duke Belloch raised his sword slowly and widened his stance.

"It's called propaganda, Oleg, and it's very useful. Now, en garde."

Oleg continued to stare at the painting across the room as he spoke, "Propaganda? You all got a funny word for painting..."

SMACK

"OWWW!" cried out Oleg as the Duke bludgeoned him in the side of the face with the blunt side of his blade.

Unprepared for the force of the blow, Oleg tumbled awkwardly down to the floor.

"Ooooooh," squealed an excited voice from across the room.

Oleg looked up from the floor and glared over at the Lord Mayor, a portly man with a golden chain around his neck that held the golden seal to the city.

"Ooooooh," squealed the Lord Mayor again. "Well done your Grace. That's another point for you. The score is now Duke Belloch fifty four, Oleg one."

"What can I say?" gloated the Duke. "I'm a master swordsman. Did I ever tell you that I was captain of the fencing club back home in Rivolli?"

Oleg rolled his eyes as he gingerly stood up. Both he and the Lord Mayor had heard this story many times before.

"Oh, do tell, your grace," encouraged the Lord Mayor with a small bow.

Duke Belloch flourished his sword, then placed it carefully in his scabbard.

"Well, not to brag," bragged Belloch. "But I did win the master's cup eight years in a row. Perhaps you'd like to hear about those matches?"

Oleg sighed ever so slightly.

"Oh yes," eagerly clapped the Lord Mayor. "It sounds quite exciting."

"Well," began the Duke. "My love for sword fighting all started when I was a young child and found my father's sword. I would use it to chase and stab any of my nannies that dared try to force a bed time upon me."

"How brave, my Grace," groveled the Lord Mayor.

"Yeah, that's great," interrupted Oleg in an annoyed tone. "But we have an issue with the peasants to deal with."

The Duke rested his hand upon the golden pommel of his sword as he prepared to listen.

"Well," continued Oleg. "As you know, your plan to take advantage of the fact that all the poor peasants' houses 'burned down' has mostly worked. They finished work on the city's new outer wall weeks ago, and it's come out great. Bigger and thicker than any in all of Rannsaka. Kinda like me."

Oleg's lame joke landed with a lifeless thud like a wet washcloth landing upon a tile floor.

"Err, ummm," resumed Oleg. "And in the last few days, they finished work on the moat around the city. All that's left is to divert some of the Grantosh river into the moat, to fill it with water."

Oleg paused for a moment, unsure of how to go on.

Duke Belloch shrugged his shoulders, "So? I know all these things. Why are you interrupting my glorious fencing tales with stories of things that I already know?"

"I think," cautiously ventured the Lord Mayor. "That what Oleg is trying to tell you is that the peasants are getting restless. In exchange for all of their free work, you promised them new homes of their own... but you've given them no new homes."

"And," added Oleg, "even if we had the peasants build the houses themselves, we don't have enough resources for that many houses."

"That's fine," responded the relieved Duke. "I thought you meant that we had a real problem. I don't want stinky peasants in my clean new capital. They've fulfilled our purposes, now dispose of them."

The Duke's voice echoed through the massive hall, fading into an awkward silence. The Lord Mayor fiddled nervously with the golden chain around his neck. Oleg's eyes unfocused and stared off into space, as though he was looking at nothing at all. In the Duke's experience that either meant that Oleg was thinking, or that he was preparing to fart.

"We could drown them," spouted out Oleg.

The Lord Mayor's faced changed in an instant from confusion to alarm. He had no problem with letting the poor die due to poverty, starvation, over working, an inability to access healthcare. Well the list of things he was willing to let the poor die of was quite long in deed, but actively killing them was a bit of a surprise to his rich delicate sensibilities.

"Go on, Oleg. I like what you have so far," encouraged Duke Belloch.

Oleg smiled widely, "Well, I can tell them that the moat has to be deeper. Then we'll get them all in the moat digging it deeper, at the same time we'll divert the river into the moat and that will drown most of them."

The Duke nodded slowly, "But what about the survivors? A few are bound to be able to build rafts of their fellow dead and survive."

Oleg thought for a moment, then clapped his hands in joy, "We build a few nice houses, and give them to the survivors. Then we can claim that everyone was going to get those. We look like we honored our word, and we put up a monument for all the dead who perished in the tragic accident. Plus you'll still have a workforce for the new mills."

"I knew I kept you on for some reason!" joyously exclaimed the Duke, slapping Oleg on the back. "Great thinking Oleg, issue the orders at once."

"Just one little point," meekly interrupted the Lord Mayor. "Technically you need my permission to issue such an order."

The Lord Mayor suddenly found that he had a pair of devious eyes looking straight in his direction.

"Which of course you have, my permission that is," stumbled the Lord Mayor.

"Excellent, then!" smiled the Duke. "I'm glad that we're all on the same page. Now Oleg, will you please show the good Lord Mayor out. I have a lot of plantation reports to go over. I'm afraid there's no rest for the wicked."

The Lord Mayor bowed slightly, bidding Duke Belloch goodbye. Oleg's footsteps echoed on the marble floor as he walked across the room. He placed a friendly hand upon the Lord Mayor's shoulder and began to guide him towards the hall's large east door.

"Ahem," the Duke cleared his throat. "The other exit, please Oleg."

Oleg nodded, changing direction and guiding the Lord Mayor out towards the balcony.

"Have you ever been on the new majestic

balcony?" asked Oleg.

"Oh no, I'd love to see it," replied the Mayor with an eager smile. "What you've done to this place is truly extravagant."

As the Lord Mayor and Oleg disappeared out onto the fifth floor balcony, Duke Belloch sat down at his desk and began to shuffle through a pile of papers. It wasn't long before he heard a scream and then a sickening crunch from beyond the balcony's open doors. The Duke looked up from his papers towards the doors, just in time to see Oleg strut joyfully back into the room.

"It's done, boss. Like you wanted."

"What?!" shouted Duke Belloch. "You oaf! You didn't kill him did you?! We needed him!"

Fear leapt up in Oleg's eyes as the words stammered out of his mouth, "Uhh... I... I... thought... you wanted me..."

"So you did kill him?! You murdered our ally! I should have you hanged for this!"

"I'm sorry. I'm so sorry, sir," desperately pleaded Oleg, holding back tears. "I thought you meant..."

Oleg's desperate pleas were cut off as Duke Belloch erupted into a robust laughter.

"Ha, ha, ha! I'm just messing with you," chuckled the Duke. "Ha, you should have seen the look on your face. Priceless, it's the little things in life that keep us going. Don't you think?"

Oleg was at a loss for words.

"The Lord Mayor was just a figure head and a 'yes man,' we don't need him anymore," explained the Duke. "When the majority of the peasants are disposed of, there won't be enough people in this town to try and fight our rule. That, and a 'yes man' is a dangerous thing. When dealing with problems, you need to face facts, not be lied to by agreeable sycophants. Don't you agree, Oleg?"

"Yes, boss."

"Tell you what," continued Duke Belloch. "It looks like we have a job opening for a mayor. How's Lord Mayor Oleg sound to you?"

The confused look upon Oleg's face instantly transformed into a beaming smile.

"Lord Mayor Oleg sounds mighty fine to me," Oleg turned his words over carefully as though he savored their taste. "Ohh! Can I get a special hat made?"

"Yes, but first issue a decree starting our 'Drown the Poor' campaign. Needless to say though, don't use that language."

Doubt crept into Oleg's greedy mind for a brief moment, "Will the people of Siztok accept me as their Lord High Mayor?"

"Of course," reassured the Duke. "The rich of Siztok are firmly behind us and by the time they might consider other options it will be too late. Like a Butarian creeping vine that has grown around a sleeping lion. By the time the lion awakes, it is already doomed."

Oleg paused for a moment in thought, "We're the vine in that analogy, right.... not the lion?"

"Yes," sighed the Duke, rolling his eyes.

"And I still get my fancy Lord Mayor hat?"

The Duke nodded solemnly.

"Awesome!" exclaimed Oleg. "Make way for Lord High Mayor Oleg. I got a bunch of poor people to drown!"

As Oleg eagerly hurried out of the room, Duke Belloch smiled contentedly to himself.

CHAPTER 13: A GIANT PROBLEM

Hungry and disheveled, Menderchuck awoke upon a dark cold dirt floor. With a slight groan and the clinking of metal, he rolled over and gingerly sat up.

"Ugghhhh, I'm not getting any younger," grunted Menderchuck, examining the stout iron manacles which bound his wrists and ankles.

The chains that connected the manacles clinked lightly as Menderchuck shook them, testing their strength. It was sadly clear that despite their weathered appearance they were of a superior construction.

"Well, this is a pretty inglorious start in fomenting a slave rebellion," sighed Menderchuck.

As dawn began to break outside, a sliver of light snuck in through a nearby window, providing a whisper of illumination. Relieved confusion replaced dread while Menderchuck glanced about the room. He was no longer trapped in the pit. He was now in a long dilapidated wood shack whose rough walls and ceiling were littered with small holes.

Sleeping all around him, crammed shoulder to shoulder, were a great mass of malnourished men, women, and children. They filled the long house's floor from wall to wall. Dirty and poorly clothed, many wore only scant rags.

Slowly, Menderchuck's eyes scanned the room, desperately hoping to find a friendly face, a friend, a cousin, or any member of his lost clan. His brief ship of hope was soon dashed against the rocky shores of reality. None of his fellow slaves were of his clan. Yet a small life boat survived the rocky shores. A green tattoo of clan Zetti here, the distinctive braided hair of clan Dervin there, the gauged ears of clan Oghul nearby, all proved that these slaves had once been members of the horse clans, just not clan Chuck.

"I wonder if they'll recognize me?" anxiously whispered Menderchuck.

The horse clans of the Steppes had a very complicated relationship with each other. At any given moment, any two clans (or more) could be found raiding each other, trading with each other, celebrating with each other, or cursing each other. And in the great enormity of the Steppes of Rannsaka, a great many clans only knew of each other through distant rumors. Each were their own traveling petty fiefdoms.

The one thing that all clans shared in common (besides a general love of looting, horse riding, fart jokes, good food, and libations) was "the Code." "The Code" simply stated: "All things are allowed between clans, but one must never, ever, ever, never, ever, not even once, just don't even think about it, involve outsiders in our conflicts or side with them."

"There's nothing to worry about. They won't out me," nervously mumbled Menderchuck.

"I'm not worried. No one betrays the Code."

His emotions hadn't quite gotten the message though.

CLANG *CLANG* *CLANG*

Rang out a distant bell, calling the slaves to their work. One by one, the sleeping men, women, and children awoke, rose to their feet, and then shuffled out through the front door. Stiffly, Menderchuck followed suit, leaving the squalid shack behind him and stepping out into the fresh morning air.

As the multitude of slaves around him began to assemble themselves into groups for work detail, Menderchuck glanced back over his shoulder towards the long slave shack. His shack had only been one of many. All arranged in a great row. Slaves poured out of each shack. Once again, Menderchuck's eyes searched desperately for any sign of his clansmen, but none were to be seen.

With a disheartened sigh, Menderchuck turned eastward. There, across a field, dominating the entire plantation grounds, back lit by the rising sun, stood the great plantation house.

"Well," gulped Menderchuck. "I best get on it."

With the clinking of chains upon his ankles, he rapidly, awkwardly waddled out in front of the assembled groups of slaves.

"My fellow horse riders!" dramatically cried out

Menderchuck, lifting up his chained wrists for all to see. "These chains can not hold us!"

A multitude of eyes stared silently back at him. Embarrassment crept up, as Menderchuck suddenly realized that only he was clapped in chains.

"Er... We are the horse clans!" shouted out Menderchuck, trying to recover by force of will alone. "We are the riders of the Steppes! We were born to conquer, not to serve!"

Menderchuck's fiery words melted in the cool dawn to an indifferent response. Undeterred, he plowed on.

"All we need is to stand together! All the horse clans as one. None will stop us then! But first we need a mighty leader. Who here is your leader?"

Menderchuck waited only a fraction of a second, before continuing, "Ah, I see, leaderless. Well then I suggest you all follow me. I will... what?"

A small girl pointed to one of the nearby slave shacks. Menderchuck's eyes widened as he witnessed a massive man duck his head in order to exit the decrepit building.

"Golgoth..." quietly mouthed Menderchuck in anxious awe.

Though Menderchuck had never met Golgoth before, he instantly knew him by sight. The legend of Golgoth the giant was almost as big as the man himself. He stood over eight feet tall, had arms the size of a full grown man's legs, and legs the size of a tree trunk. It was said that he could eat an entire goat in a single sitting, and that he could crush rocks with his bare hands. No man or creature had ever defeated the giant in personal combat.

"You!" shouted Menderchuck, pointing toward the giant.

Golgoth paused for a confused moment beside the shack, pointing a finger back at himself.

"Yes, you!" aggressively cried out Menderchuck. "Golgoth, chief of clan Dervin, I challenge you to combat!"

Calmly, Golgoth the giant strode across the slave camp toward Menderchuck.

"Yes, you, you big, eerrrr, you are a big one," gulped Menderchuck as the approaching Golgoth towered over him.

Bewildered, Golgoth stared down at the oddly aggressive chained stranger who stood before him.

"I can smell your stink pants from here!" goaded Menderchuck. "These people deserve a better leader than you, gigantor! I challenge you for right of chieftain!"

Standing there in quiet thought, Golgoth said nothing. For you see, the giant was not used to people challenging him. Most were smart enough to try to stay on his good side.

"Fight me, you wusssssssss bucket!" taunted Menderchuck, trying to illicit a response from the towering giant.

"But, you got chains on," replied a confused Golgoth.

"I'll still whip you. Fight me, or everyone will know that you're really a giant coward!"

Golgoth shrugged indifferently, "Alright, if that's what you want."

Menderchuck's mind raced, "He's got the power, but I got speed. I just have to be fast..."

SMASH

Golgoth's fist slammed into the side of Menderchuck's head, flipping Menderchuck's body in a limp cartwheel. With a clinking of chains and a thud, Menderchuck's body collapsed onto the ground into a puddle of mud. As stars danced around his eyes, he heard the sound of laughter and cheering. He had a feeling that the cheering wasn't for him.

"I'm not done with you yet," groaned the breathless Menderchuck into the mud puddle.

"Are you serious?" incredulously asked the giant.

Menderchuck gulped and swallowed something hard, hoping to the gods that it wasn't a tooth. Shaky, covered in mud, he climbed to his feet, stumbling back towards Golgoth. Aggressively, Menderchuck poked his finger into the giant's chest, leaving a muddy fingerprint.

"You," spat out Menderchuck. "You're going down, Golgoth, just like your cow of a mother."

In retrospect, Menderchuck would later admit that it was a mean and, more importantly, stupid thing to say. Golgoth's mother had been a lovely woman, and the giant did not take insults to her lightly.

"ARRRR!" roared out Golgoth, lifting Menderchuck in one swift motion.

"Wait, wait, wait!" sputtered Menderchuck. "Maybe we can talk about this!"

Furious, Golgoth raised Menderchuck high above his head, pivoted to face a slave shack, then hurled Menderchuck towards a window. Well Golgoth had meant to throw Menderchuck through a window, but he missed.

Menderchuck's body flew through the air, crashing head first into the side of the building with a loud crack and a wet fart. For Menderchuck, the world went black as his body rag dolled to the ground.

CHAPTER 14: THE WORK FIELDS

An old black crow arched his weathered wings, gliding high above the plantation's massive east wheat fields. Though the old crow was usually quite proud of his black plumage, on a day like today, he almost wished that the great creator had given him wings of a lighter cooler color.

While oppressive heat waves rolled off of the noonday sun, high above him, the old crow gazed curiously down at the wheat fields far below. There he saw men who rode on horses. They wore purple uniforms upon their bodies with truncheons and whips at their sides. Lazily, they watched over a multitude of malnourished men, women, and children who were busily slaving away, cutting wheat.

For a moment, the old crow pondered to himself, wondering what could possibly motivate the humans below to be out working on such a miserable day. The moment was short lived though, for the old crow had learned long ago that trying to apply logic to the actions of humans only resulted in headaches and confusion.

Torfulson, wearing a guard uniform and sitting upon a brown mare, took little notice of the old crow who flew overhead.

"Please be here somewhere," anxiously muttered Torfulson, shielding his eyes with a hand as he hurriedly scanned the east wheat fields.

Time, you see, was not on Torfulson's side. Foreman Collin's had specifically ordered Torfulson to check in with the kitchen and report back on tonight's dinner menu, and it was not wise to displease the foreman. Instead though, Torfulson had taken a quick detour to the east fields to try and find his father.

"Oh, thank the gods," gasped Torfulson, laying his eyes upon his father who stood a hundred feet away on the edge of a group of slaves.

Instantly, Torfulson spurred his horse into a full gallop.

"This is so much easier with a saddle," thought Torfulson, feet firmly in the stirrups, hands gripping the reins as the brown mare flew across the field.

Though Torfulson was growing fond of the brown mare, in reality, he missed his ass. And he hoped, that where ever Muffin the Slayer of Souls was now, that she was enjoying a nice carrot and a cool drink of water.

More than a few slaves jealously glanced up, watching Torfulson and horse speed by, longing for the bygone days in which they too had freely rode the plains.

Sweat pouring from his brow, pain shooting down his back, scythe firmly in hand, Menderchuck twisted his upper body, felling the wheat before him.

"Cut down in its prime," Menderchuck forlornly whispered to himself, remembering his clan's destruction at Duke Belloch's hand.

It was then that Menderchuck heard a horse skid to a halt behind him. With an inaudible sigh, he dutifully continued his work.

"Slave!" cried out a deep commanding voice from behind him. "You missed a spot over there!"

The truth is, Menderchuck had missed many spots. He wasn't particularly skilled in cutting wheat.

"Yes, master," obediently replied Menderchuck, turning towards the voice. "I'll get right on it... you bastard! Torf!"

With a hearty laugh, Torfulson quickly dismounted his horse. Reins in hand, he stepped closer to Menderchuck so that they could converse in private.

"Where have you been?!" demanded Menderchuck.

"This place is huge. They keep assigning me to the north fields. The foreman told me to head to the kitchens, but I took a quick detour. I've been looking for you for all day."

"Well you found me," replied Menderchuck, wiping the sweat from his dirty brow.

Torfulson took a white handkerchief from his

shirt pocket and wiped some sweat from his own brow.

"Man, it's hot today," declared Torfulson, replacing the handkerchief and pulling his canteen off of his shoulder.

"Yeah, must be real difficult sitting upon a horse and watching people work," sarcastically responded Menderchuck, eyes transfixed upon the canteen.

Torfulson lifted the canteen to his lips and took a big refreshing swig of water. More than a few thirsty slaves cast jealous gazes in his direction. As Torfulson wiped the excess water from his lips, he noticed Menderchuck's stare.

"You want a drink?" asked Torfulson, offering his canteen to his father.

The chains around Menderchuck's feet clinked softly. Quickly, he took a half step forward, greedily grabbing the canteen. In one swift move, the barbarian raised the canteen to his parched lips, tilting it upward. *glug* *glug* Two gulps were all that he could manage, before the canteen ran dry.

"Ugh, What the butts, Torf?" cried out Menderchuck. "Save some for the rest of us, you water glutton."

"Sorry, I've been sneaking drinks to your fellow slaves."

"Oh..." stuttered Menderchuck, handing the

empty canteen back to his son.

"Sooo?" eagerly asked Torfulson. "Did you find your... errr our clan? Are they ready to rise up in rebellion?"

"Not exactly..."

"What's that mean?"

"No," flatly stated Menderchuck.

"No, what?"

"No, none of our clan is here," explained Menderchuck. "And... no, no one is ready to follow me in rebellion."

"What have you been doing this whole time?!" blurted out Torfulson.

"Ummm, being a slave," sassily retorted Menderchuck. "That's kinda a full time gig! Maybe you should try it sometime!"

Menderchuck's voice rang out through the east field, drawing more than a few curious gazes.

"Sorry, sorry," hurriedly whispered Torfulson. "You're right. I'm out of line. So what do we do now?"

Menderchuck pointed toward a giant slave, who was busily cutting wheat, about fifty feet away.

"I attacked that man," announced Menderchuck.

"What?! Why?" groaned the increasingly confused Torfulson.

"That's Golgoth, chief of clan Dervin. I challenged him for the title of chieftain, by right of combat."

A quiet lull came over father and son as the two men stared at each other.

"And?!" blinked Torfulson. "What happened? Did you win?"

Silently, Menderchuck parted the hair upon his head, revealing a massive welt.

"UhhhhhHHH!" groaned Torfulson. "Are there other tribes you can lead? There's a lot of horse riders here."

"Well," postulated Menderchuck. "Maybe... There's a fair amount of folks from clans Zetti, Oghul, Tenzing, Vi..."

"Great!" interrupted Torfulson. "Go fight one of them for chieftain."

"I can't do that."

"Why not?!" gasped Torfulson, running his nervous fingers through his hair.

"That's not how those clans work," explained Menderchuck. "It's different for different clans. For us, clan Chuck, leaders are determined by right of birth. Clan Tenzing is the same, but I doubt I can rightly climb up into to their matron's womb, squirt out, and yell 'Behold your new chief!'"

Torfulson shuddered and winced, wishing his imagination wasn't quite so vivid.

"Clan Oghul values intellect and history," continued Menderchuck. "Their leaders are chosen from those who can best recite their historic epics. Talk about boring. And clan Zetti values horsemanship most. If I recall correctly, they use horse races to determine clan hierarchy. Oh, can you get us some horses?"

"Definitely not," replied Torfulson, shaking his head. "That's like the most important rule of being a guard, don't let the horse riders get access to horses. If I did that, I'd instantly be fired, or worse yet, revealed."

While Torfulson talked on, Menderchuck froze in place. Menderchuck's anxious eyes looked past his son toward a man who was riding upon a black stallion. It was foreman Collins, and he was fast approaching.

"Hit me," brusquely commanded Menderchuck, interrupting Torfulson's monologue.

"What if you tried a foot race... what? UFFFFFFF!!!" painfully gasped Torfulson as Menderchuck suddenly bent down below the wheat line and elbowed his son in the crotch.

Torfulson's arms flew forward out of protective reflex. At the same moment, Menderchuck slapped himself as hard as he could on the side of his own face, yelling out in fake pain. The crack of the slap and Menderchuck's pain filled holler carried across the wheat fields.

Torfulson's face flushed red with pain filled rage. Clenching his hand into a fist, he pulled his arm back, determined to punch Menderchuck.

"What is going on here?!" demanded foreman Collins.

Torfulson stopped cold, startled by the unexpected voice behind him. At the same moment, foreman Collins menacingly pulled his iron truncheon from his belt.

"Sorry Master," Menderchuck apologetically blurted out to Torfulson. "I'm sorry, I'm sorry, I just wanted a little rest. I'll get right back to cutting, just please stop beating me."

Menderchuck bent to a knee, picking up the scythe and purposely turning his head away from the foreman, revealing a red hand mark across the side of his face.

"Nothing sir," squeaked Torfulson in a high pitched voice, spinning to face the foreman before clearing his throat and recovering himself. "Nothing sir, that I can't handle."

From atop his black stallion, foreman Collins' eyes squinted, staring down upon Menderchuck. Then he turned to face Torfulson, who stood there in silent terror at the thought of being discovered.

"Aren't you supposed to be in the kitchen?" coldly inquired foreman Collins.

"Yes sir, sorry sir," answered Torfulson. "On my way there, I saw this slave slacking, and I made a little detour to correct the situation. I apologize."

Foreman Collins toyed with the iron truncheon in his grasp, gazing off towards the great plantation house.

"Quite a bit of a detour," firmly declared the foreman. "Wouldn't you say?"

"Y..yes sir," replied Torfulson, thinking on his feet. "But just look at that horribly cut wheat, you can see that from a mile away."

Torfulson pointed to one of the many wheat stalks that stood in small lonely islands. Spots that Menderchuck had missed in his cutting.

"Hmph," grunted the foreman, staring at the wheat stalks. "Slave! Are you blind?"

"No master," groveled Menderchuck, hard at work.

"Well, you could have fooled me," grunted foreman Collins.

Torfulson forced a weak smile onto his face.

"Alright, guard, get to the kitchen," commanded the foreman.

"Yes sir," nodded Torfulson, leaping up upon his brown mare.

As Torfulson rode off toward the great plantation house, foreman Collins guided his black stallion closer to Menderchuck.

"And you," threatened the foreman, shoving his boot into Menderchuck's back. "Clean up that cutting. There's little room here for useless slaves."

CHAPTER 15:
TORFULSON THE GUARD

squish *squish* *squish* Echoed out the squishy sounds of Torfulson's muddy boots upon the grand plantation house's hard marble floor. As he crossed the foyer, he left a trail of muddy boot prints in his wake. An elderly house slave, mop in hand, gave Torfulson the guard a sidelong look, but dared not say a word.

"Sorry..." weakly apologized Torfulson, passing to left of the grand staircase's banisters, through an archway, out of the foyer, and into a side hallway.

The lonely sounds of Torfulson's footsteps were his only companions as he walked the length of the hall, ignoring the gilded paintings which hung from the pristine white walls around him. As he crossed in front of an open side door, he heard the murmur of conversation and then the shouting of a familiar voice.

"Torfy!" called out Glenn. "You gotta get in here!"

squish Torfulson hesitantly came to a stop, glancing through the open doorway into the large sunlit room. On the far side of the room, his eyes beheld great windows, bound by iron frames, which rose to the ceiling. A row of tables, with men sitting behind them, rested near the base of the windows. And in front of each table, there stood a multitude of guards, each patiently waiting in parallel lines. Glenn burst forth from one of the lines, rushing toward the open door.

"Where have you been?" demanded Glenn, grabbing Torfulson by the arm and dragging him into the room. "You almost missed the most important day of the month."

"I... I did?" replied a very confused Torfulson, glancing nervously at the multitude of guards which filled the room around him.

"Most definitely," added Glenn, leading Torfulson toward the front of the line.

"Hey!" shouted an angry guard from a nearby line. "You two, go to the back, you can't cut in line."

"Oh, I can't?" Glenn's words came out like cold steel, his eyes shooting daggers toward the other guard. "I'll tell you what, Vick. How about you shut your whore mouth, or I'll gut you in your sleep."

"Oh yeah?!" challenged Vick, his hackles raised. "If you're a man, then come get me, short stuff."

"I'm not short!" screamed Glenn, the veins on his neck popping out.

The murmur of conversation died as all eyes turned toward Glenn and Vick. Glenn furrowed his brow for a moment, then glanced over his shoulder toward a taller guard who stood directly behind him.

"Adam," declared Glenn.

Adam shook his head disapprovingly, sighed, then turned toward Vick.

"Vick," commanded Adam. "Shut up."

"Oh looook," taunted Vick. "Glenn has to get his wife to defend him."

As laughter erupted from the assembled mass, Adam burst forward, crossing the distance from his line to Vick's in two quick strides. With one forceful hand, Adam wrapped his fingers firmly around Vick's wrist. Vick's face grimaced. His hand trembled, fighting in vain to resist Adam's grasp. Slowly, Adam lifted Vick's hand up to face level.

"Le... Let me go!" gasped Vick.

With a cold deliberateness, Adam's free hand grasped one of Vick's fingers, bending it backward until it made a gut wrenching popping sound.

"AGGGGHHHH," screamed out Vick in immense pain, his finger dangling loosely from his hand.

"Shut up, Vick," calmly repeated Adam with a cruel smile on his face, before slowly turning around and returning to his former spot in line.

"I saw 'him' again last night," declared Glenn, grinning at what had just transpired.

"Doubt it," scoffed Adam. "You were probably just dreaming."

"I wasn't dreaming!" protested Glenn. "I really saw him! I've seen him twice now, clear as day... only it was at night!"

Adam rolled his eyes while a frustrated Glenn turned towards Torfulson.

"You believe me, that I saw him, right Torfy?"

"Saw who?" asked Torfulson.

"Menderchuck, the barbarian king."

Torfulson's blood ran cold upon hearing his father's name.

"He's one of the greatest horse tribe barbarian kings," explained Glenn. "Last night, under the full moon, as I stood guard duty, I saw him off in the distance, riding on his majestic horse. He probably saw me and was scared off."

To Glenn's dismay, he heard Adam burst into laughter behind him.

"What?" demanded Glenn, stomping his feet as the line moved forward.

"So, you're telling me," asked Adam between chuckles. "That the ghost of a great barbarian king saw you, got scared, and ran off?"

"Yes! Maybe!.. What, what ghost?"

"Menderchuck is dead, you moron," laughed Adam.

"Next," declared a man who sat at the table before them.

"Then what about the rumors from Tserkva?" indignantly pouted Glenn. "They say that Menderchuck was seen there some time past, buying horses from Evander's."

"NEXT," repeated the seated man.

"Why does a dead man need a horse?" asked Adam.

"I... I don't know," sputtered Glenn. "He prob..."

"GLENN!" shouted out the seated man from the table. "Quit holding up the line! Get your lazy butt up here."

"Ooooh," smiled Glenn. "We're next."

Eagerly, Glenn grabbed Torfulson by the shoulder, dragging him up to the table.

"Glenn and Torfy," brightly declared Glenn to the seated man.

With an exasperated sigh, the seated man began to studiously run a finger down the great ledger which rested on the table before him.

"Uh... maybe I should go," weakly suggested Torfulson, trying to step away.

"Nonsense," disputed Glenn, grabbing Torfulson's arm and holding him in place.

"Glenn, Glenn..... Glenn, there you are," murmured the man, before dipping his pen in ink and marking a check next to the name. "And what was your name again?"

The man looked up from the ledger, squinting with judgmental eyes at Torfulson.

"Torfulson," squeaked Torfulson.

"Hmmm," grunted the man, returning to the ledger.

Though the lines around them moved ever forward, time stood still for Torfulson. With each page that the man examined, each line of names that he carefully combed through, fear crept up Torfulson's spine, pleading with him to run.

"I don't see your name here," announced the man. "Are you even supposed to be here, son?"

"Of course he is!" interrupted Glenn. "He's been here for two weeks, kicking slave booty into booty pie."

"Is that true?" coldly asked the man, staring up at Torfulson.

"Yesss," weakly lied Torfulson. "Ummm, except maybe about the booty pie. I don't know what that is."

The man looked Torfulson up and down, carefully studying him.

"Huh," grunted the man, clearing his throat. "Welll... I'm sorry son, must be a clerical error."

The man then dipped his pen into his ink bottle and scrawled Torfulson's name into the ledger.

"We've had so many new faces coming in over the last few months that this happens from time to time," explained the man, reaching into a leather pouch and pulling out six gold guilder coins.

Four coins he placed in Glenn's greedy outstretched hand, and two he placed into Torfulson's surprised hand. For a moment, Torfulson wondered at the shiny gold within his grasp.

"Holy crap," muttered Torfulson. "That's more than I used to make in an entire month as a milk mai... ma... man! Milk man, delivering milk."

Glenn smiled, giving Torfulson a friendly slap on the shoulder.

"The work is crap, but the pay is great," exclaimed Glenn. "Adam, get your pay, then we getting some drinks! You're in too, right Torfy?"

Torfulson smiled ever so slightly and nodded in agreement. After such a horrible couple of weeks, drinks with the boys sounded good, and that was the most insidious part of it all. For the first time in his life, Torfulson felt like a part of the group. And though he was loath to admit it to himself, deep down inside, a small part of him liked the feeling.

CHAPTER 16: DUKE BELLOCH

Sunlight poured in through the glass balcony doors of what had once been St. Ufstath's cathedral's fifth floor hall. Particles of dust floated lazily in the rays of light. The quiet sounds of shuffling papers drifted through the massive hall past walls covered in swords, shields, suits of armor, majestic paintings of battles, and a multitude of hunting trophies.

The source of the shuffling sounds came from a massive oak desk on the far end of the hall. The desk was large enough and stout enough that it could have served as a gnome's ship. Its sides were carved with victorious images of Duke Belloch in combat. Its top was covered with a multitude of papers. Plantation reports, army reports, quartermaster reports, and the rare unopened letter from his wife.

Duke Belloch sat at his grand desk, staring blankly at the papers before him. Try as he might, he was unable to focus upon their contents. The part of his brain that usually reveled in plantation production numbers was much too distracted. Time and time again, his eyes drifted over toward a small crudely written letter which sat alone on the far corner of his desk. For the better part of an hour, he had tried to put the letter out of mind. Yet, stubbornly, resolutely, it had remained firmly embedded in his thoughts, pushing out all else.

"Oleg! Someone bring me Oleg!" cried out Duke Belloch, finally giving in to his nagging concerns.

A few minutes later, Oleg appeared in the hall's large east doorway. In his right hand was a large cooked turkey leg. Grease covered his hand and his beard.

"You wanted me?" asked Oleg, but it sounded more like, "Uffff wafen meef?"

"Don't speak with your mouthful, you oaf."

Oleg spit out his mouthful of turkey. It landed upon the marble floor with a wet thud.

"My name's Oleg, not oaf," densely corrected Oleg.

Duke Belloch glared at the disgusting lump of chewed turkey which now sullied his beautiful marble floor.

"Uhh..., Uhhh... sorry boss," quickly apologized Oleg, scurrying over toward the mess.

With his free hand, Oleg bent down and picked up the chuck of pre-chewed turkey. Then he stood there awkwardly for a moment, holding it, before finally deciding to put it into one of his pockets. The Duke sighed dismissively to see such a sight, then lifted the small letter from the corner of his desk.

"Do you know what I hold here?" coldly asked the Duke.

"It's paper," smugly smiled Oleg. "I know that

one! I like this game. What else you got?"

"Don't be stupid!" shouted the Duke. "I don't pay you to be stupid. I am perfectly capable of being stupid on my own, thank you."

Duke Belloch wasn't quite sure that his words had come out the way that he had intended, but he was sure that now was not the time to correct it.

"It's supposedly a letter from one of my guards named Glenn or perhaps Gleen. It's hard to tell. His spelling is atrocious," explained the Duke. "He claims that he saw Menderchuck the terrible riding upon his mighty whores, I can only assume that he means horse, the other night."

Oleg's eyes widened as he tightly clenched his fist around the turkey leg.

"Clearly," continued Duke Belloch. "This guard is misinformed. As we all know, you killed Menderchuck in battle. So I might as well toss rubbish this, don't you think?"

"Yes, let's not give it another thought," rapidly agreed Oleg.

Oleg's eyes were transfixed upon the paper as Duke Belloch slowly lifted it above a nearby trash bin. For a moment, the Duke relaxed his grip, causing the letter to tilt downward toward the trash.

"Funny though," added the Duke, suddenly

tightening his grip upon the paper. "The letter mentions one more thing."

"Probably should just toss it," muttered Oleg.

"Our new friend Glenn also claims that Menderchuck was rather recently seen buying horses from Evander," coolly explained Belloch. "But that's probably just a salacious rumor."

"Definitely a salamander rumor," agreed Oleg, rapidly nodding his head.

"I thought so too," slyly continued the Duke. "Exxxxcept, I had some of my men ask around town and apparently they've heard the rumor too. So, Oleg, what do you think we should do?"

"Ummm," sheepishly mumbled Oleg. "Throw away the letter?"

"We could," smugly agreed Duke Belloch. "Or you could try telling me the truth. Do the dead now walk the earth in search of livestock bargains as they rebuild their clans and seek revenge? Or are the rumors are false? Can you guarantee that Menderchuck is dead?"

"Probably dead," sheepishly replied Oleg .

The red hot flames of anger flashed in Duke Belloch's eyes.

"The thing is," desperately lied Oleg. "I bested him in battle. I chopped him up and left him there, lying on the ground, bleeding, dying."

Duke Belloch's eyes blinked, staring incredulously back at Oleg.

"I don't know," muttered Oleg. "Maybe he got better."

"You know what I think," uttered Belloch through gritted teeth. "I think you were too busy greedily enslaving your friends and family to see if one of our biggest threats was dead."

"Ummm, is it bad if I say yes?" meekly answered Oleg.

Duke Belloch crushed the letter in his hand, balling his fingers into a fist.

"Go," quietly commanded a furious Duke. "Go and get Evander. Bring him here so that we may question him."

"Yes sir!"

"Oh, and Oleg," added Duke Belloch. "If the horse merchant is found dead, then you will soon follow."

Oleg nodded, spun around, and began to walk out of the room. As he did, he reached into his pocket and pulled out the partially chewed lump of turkey. With one swift motion, he popped it back into his mouth and began to anxiously chew it once again.

"Go faster!" exclaimed the Duke.

With an awkward stumble, Oleg sped up,

scurrying out of the room.

CHAPTER 17: HURRY UP

The early glow of dawn snuck over the eastern horizon spreading its weak light over the plantation. Near the dilapidated slave quarters, the slaves stood quietly in line waiting for foreman Collins to arrive. The world was still dark when they were first called to order over half an hour ago. Hurry up and wait was the way that the foreman ran the plantation.

As he stood there silently, Menderchuck looked up and down the line of his fellow slaves. He was most amazed by the parents who managed to keep their children quiet for so long. Obviously they feared a beating from the guards, but nonetheless, keeping children quiet for so long was a super human feat.

Menderchuck snapped back to attention when he heard the clip clop of hooves slowly approach. The foreman road upon a great black stallion. Menderchuck's brows furrowed in revulsion at the sight of such an unworthy man riding upon such a noble creature.

"Alright horse raiders," derisively declared foreman Collins. "Good news, Morthi died last night. He was standing behind a horse and *pop* it kicked his lights out."

Many of the slaves quietly frowned, including Menderchuck. Horse riders learned as young children to never stand directly behind a horse. The odds were very unlikely that Morthi had been killed by a horse kick.

Menderchuck glanced toward the foreman's waist and saw a more likely culprit, an iron bar. Most of the guards carried wooden truncheons to keep the slaves in line. Foreman Collins carried one made of iron.

"Soooo," foreman Collins smiled. "We have an opening for horse duty. Who would like it?"

Menderchuck's hand shot up almost instinctively. He would have done almost anything to get out of field work for even a single day. And the thought of working with horses again brought a flicker of joy to his dark and troubled soul.

"Oh, I do like an eager beaver," declared the foreman, looking at Menderchuck's raised hand. "The job is yours. Report to the barns. The rest of you, to the fields."

Menderchuck smiled dumbly with his hand still in the air. As he turned around to look at his fellow slaves, he noticed for the first time that none of the other slaves had raised their hands.

CHAPTER 18: HORSE DUTY

squish *plop* Menderchuck scooped up another shovelful of horse manure.

"Ugh," he groaned.

Horse duty was not what Menderchuck had envisioned it'd be. He had wistfully dreamed of feeding and brushing down the plantation's horses. Sadly though, there weren't even any horses here. They were much too busy in the fields, carrying guards upon their backs.

Menderchuck stepped out of the great barn's dark interior, beneath the high hayloft above, and into the bright morning sun. Carefully balancing the shovelful of manure before him, he walked past one of the barn's great double doors, which stood wide open, to a waiting horse cart. Horseless, the cart stood alone, holding a pile of fresh horse droppings in its open bed. With a small grunt, Menderchuck lifted the shovel up toward the cart. Suddenly, his hands moved forward, but the shovel refused to follow, tipping out of his hands, dumping manure onto the grass below.

"UGH!" grunted Menderchuck, pulling angrily on the shovel to no avail.

But the shovel refused to budge for its handle had snagged upon a chain. A thick iron chain, with a great iron lock, hung from the handle of the barn's nearby door. In fury, Menderchuck grabbed the chain, trying to tear it from the door handle, but it held fast to the door.

"You stupid poop chain!" cursed Menderchuck.

Try as he might, the barbarian could not wrench the chain from the door handle and this was for good reason. Each night, the barn was locked fast by guard to prevent the enslaved horse riders from procuring a mount that might lead them to freedom.

"Having a problem?" asked a voice that seemed to be grinning.

Surprised, Menderchuck spun to face the voice. There he saw his son Torfulson, dressed in the guard's purple, sitting upon a brown mare. Instantly, the fury melted from Menderchuck's face, replaced by a weary smile.

"We don't have much time," whispered Torfulson, bringing his horse alongside his father. "I brought them here, do your thing."

Torfulson pointed to a ragtag group of slaves that were walking towards the barn. The enslaved horse riders numbered about a dozen and were lead by Golgoth the giant with his loyal friend Enok at his side.

"Do what thing?" groaned Menderchuck, staring off at the approaching giant.

"You know, what we talked about the other day," hurriedly whispered Torfulson. "I know this is a mixed work detail, but this one had the most of the green tattoo people, the uhhh...

zebras?"

"Zetti," corrected Menderchuck, still gazing worriedly at Golgoth.

"Yeah, yeah, that's what I said. Now hurry, I can only leave them here for a few minutes before I have to take them to the east fields."

Before Menderchuck could argue, Torfulson had already spurred his horse, galloping off towards the plantation house. Thinking quickly, Menderchuck freed the shovel's handle from the iron chain then quickly approached his fellow slaves.

"Greetings, Zetti, right?" asked Menderchuck, ignoring Golgoth and engaging the half dozen plus men who wore green tattoos of various shapes.

"Yes," replied one who had a green coiled snake tattooed upon his arm. "I'm Sven, and you are?"

"I'm the man who would like to meet your chief," beamed Menderchuck.

Like a fall storm, a dark heavy cloud crossed the faces of the tattooed men.

"We have no chief," explained Sven, his eyes miles away from his voice.

"Duke Belloch?"

The men nodded in silent agreement to Menderchuck's words. Those, who have suffered life's deepest cuts, need not always speak aloud to share deep sentiments.

"You have my sympathies," spoke Menderchuck from the heart.

He glanced toward the distant plantation house. There he saw Torfulson dismounting his ride. Time was short.

"So," postulated Menderchuck, already knowing the answer full well. "Is it true you decide your chief by right of horse race?"

"Yes," agreed Sven. "That is our way."

"Well then, I challenge you to a race for right of chieftain."

"We have no horses," disputed Sven. "We can not race."

"I guess you're right," concurred Menderchuck. "But, we do have feet. We could do a foot race."

"No, that is not our way," replied Sven as the tattooed men behind him shook their heads.

"That's fair," coyly agreed Menderchuck. "If clan Zetti is too cowardly to race on foot for chieftain, then I will respect that."

Pride is an odd cargo, easily afforded by rich and poor alike. The weight of it can bring a man to ruin, yet even the weakest of people can carry great multitudes of it with them wherever they go. And for clan Zetti, it was no different.

119

Quickly, the half dozen plus green tattooed horse riders huddled up, trading whispers amongst themselves.

"Your challenge is accepted," smiled Sven, stepping from the huddle with a prideful smile upon his face. "You will face me. The fastest man our clan has ever birthed."

"Excellent!" erupted Menderchuck. "Ok, this will be the finish line."

Menderchuck drew a line in the dirt with the blade of his shovel.

"Follow me," commanded Menderchuck.

With Sven in tow, Menderchuck stepped off thirty paces then drew another line in the dirt.

"And this is the starting line," explained Menderchuck.

Sven nodded his approval as both men took their marks behind the starting line.

"I'll bet my dinner on the Zetti!" declared Enok, hopeful for a taker.

"Done," agreed Golgoth to Enok's surprise.

Golgoth's giant hand enveloped Enok's as the friends shook on the bet.

"Hey pipsqueak!" commanded Menderchuck. "If you fun boys are done holding hands, then maybe you could count us down."

Enok shot a disapproving glare toward Menderchuck, then began the countdown.

"THREE"

"You going to run with that?" asked Sven, glancing at the shovel which rested upon Menderchuck's shoulder.

"Yup," replied Menderchuck, knees bending.

"TWO"

"Nawwww, really?" wondered Sven, leaning slightly over the starting line.

"Yup," explained Menderchuck. "It's my lucky running shovel. As long as I hold it, I've never lost a race."

"ONE"

"Really? How's it work?"

"Like this," grunted Menderchuck.

In one swift motion, Menderchuck brought the flat side of the shovel down upon Sven's head. *clang* Rang out the shovel as Sven collapsed to the ground like a sack of potatoes.

"GO!"

Shovel in hand, Menderchuck burst across the starting line, leaving the unconscious Sven on the ground behind him. Feet churning, lungs gasping, Menderchuck sped (to the best of his ability) across the race course. The crowd watched in shock as Menderchuck finally crossed the finish line, claiming victory.

"Cheater!" shouted out Enok, approaching Menderchuck. "Cheater! You can't do that!"

"Why not?" asked Menderchuck.

"You attacked your opponent," argued Enok. "You killed him!"

Both men looked back across the race path to the starting line. There they saw Sven's limp body upon the ground.

"Oh, he's fine," disputed Menderchuck. "Look, he's moving."

It was true, Sven's body was twitching ever so slightly like an injured deer.

"Oh no, you lost!" quarreled Enok.

"Did I though?" smugly smiled Menderchuck, lifting his shovel high above his head in celebration. "Clan Zetti, let's hear it for your new chieftain!"

To Enok's utter dismay, a joyous cheer arose from the horse riders who wore green tattoos.

"Looks like someone owes me their dinner tonight," grinned Golgoth, placing a friendly hand upon Enok's shoulder.

Enok angrily pulled his shoulder from the giant's

grasp.

"This is horse crap," pouted Enok.

"All's fair in love, and Zetti races," explained Golgoth with a chuckle.

As the smattering of cheers rose up, so too did a feeling that Menderchuck had long missed. The pride of leading seasoned warriors.

"Golgoth," declared Menderchuck, hand offered in friendship. "Join us, together our clans shall overthrow our oppressors."

Golgoth dismissively looked over to the half dozen plus members of clan Zetti and shook his head.

"Alright then," announced Menderchuck. "Golgoth, chief of clan Dervin, I challenge you to combat for right of chieftain!"

"No," scoffed the giant. "I will not fight you again."

"Come on. Fight me, ugly," taunted Menderchuck.

Golgoth frowned, "You know you don't have to be mean. I maybe a giant, but I'm still a person. I have feelings too. Giant feelings."

"To bad you're not giant in your pants, where it counts," teased Menderchuck.

And with that, Golgoth the giant turned his back

to Menderchuck the barbarian and began to walk away.

"Fight me!" shouted Menderchuck, lifting his shovel up and charging Golgoth.

CRACK Menderchuck brought the shovel down hard upon the giant's back. To his horror, the shovel's handle cracked in two, as though it had collided with a brick wall. With a furious grunt, the giant slowly turned toward Menderchuck.

"Now... um... now..." pleaded Menderchuck, backing up. "Maybe we shoul.... aggghhhkkk"

The giant wrapped his fingers around Menderchuck's throat, lifting him high into the air. Face turning purple, Menderchuck struggled in vain against the giant's grasp while the giant strode across the barnyard toward the manure cart. In one fluid motion, the giant effortlessly tossed Menderchuck as though he were a small bag. Menderchuck's body arched through the air.

"HUHHH," gasped in Menderchuck, desperate for air.

Instantly, he regretted opening his mouth to breathe, landing face first in the manure pile that he had spent all morning piling up.

"I guess you could say that he's in a crappy situation," quipped Enok.

Golgoth just shook his head and sighed.

CHAPTER 19: OGHUL

The weary swishing sounds of a hundred scythes, cutting the golden wheat of the immense west field, hung heavily in the thick afternoon air. The main culprit for the horrible humidity lay to the northwest, well beyond the multitude of slaves who stood in vast lines harvesting grain, just beyond the boundaries of the plantation grounds, hidden in a small forest that sat north of the plantation's main road. There, a small river snaked between the forest's elder trees, flowing out into the plains beyond.

On a good day, the river cooled the forest, feeding its lush plant life, and quenching the thirst of its tiny furry animal inhabitants. But today was not a good day. Being a river, it had traveled far and wide while also resting perfectly still in bed. It had had a million roaring conversations with a great distant river and a thousand babbling chats with hundreds of nearer brooks and creeks.

And to be quite frank, the small river had grown very weary, weary of the deluge of atrocities that it heard about on a daily basis, weary of the injustices that it often witnessed beside its very banks. And today, it had had too much. In an indignant huff that had lasted the better part of the day, the small river threw a great quantity of moisture into the air, covering the Westernson plantation with a thick blanket of oppressive humidity.

"Uhhhghhh," grunted Menderchuck, wiping

125

the profuse sweat from his brow.

His efforts, though, amounted to little. Almost instantly, the sweat had returned in even greater quantities. Menderchuck's eyes darted about in search of attentive guards. At least two dozen armed guards, riding upon horses, patrolled the vast west field.

"Come on, come on," impatiently whispered Menderchuck, watching and waiting for the nearest guard to avert his gaze.

The moment that the guard had turned away, Menderchuck lifted his scythe, ducked down below the wheat, and darted across the field towards the nearest work group.

"Ohh, my knees. I'm too old for this," lamented a frustrated Menderchuck.

He had spent the majority of the work day in this cycle. Sneaking from slave work group to slave work group, searching in vain for something. Each clandestine trip fraught with the peril of discovery. Each covert journey bringing the hope for that which he sought, only to end in disappointment. And so, with fatigued legs and a greatly fatigued soul, he began to approach another work group from behind.

A long line of wheat sheaves covered the ground in parallel lines leading to the work group. Upon the ground, ten feet ahead, a young boy gathered stalks of wheat, tying them into sheaves. Another ten feet beyond, a small group of poorly fed slaves stood in a wide line, mowing

126

the wheat before them.

Hoisting his scythe onto his shoulder, Menderchuck rushed forward towards the work detail. As the sound of fallen wheat rapidly crunched under foot, Menderchuck glanced down at the work boy. The boy wore a soiled shirt upon his body and ragged unkempt hair upon his head. Clumsily, he tied the gathered wheat into sheaves. It was then that Menderchuck's eyes lit up with hope. The boy's earlobes were round with a sizable hole in the middle. With a polite smile and a nod that the boy returned, Menderchuck flew past the child toward the rest of the work group.

"Where is she? Where is she?" hastily whispered Menderchuck to himself, surveying the slaves before him. "No... No... wait, that's gotta be her!"

The woman stood a head shorter than Menderchuck. Upon her head she wore a tied piece of cloth, and upon her body she wore rough patched leather that must have been a jerkin in a former life. The exposed skin of her arms and face were tanned by the Steppes' harsh sun and covered in the scars of battle. And her earlobes, the part that Menderchuck seemed most interested in, were marked by the telltale iron ring of the Oghul gauge. Diligently, she swung her scythe before her, cutting as she walked.

"Are you Inju, great chieftess of the Oghul?" asked Menderchuck, sidling up beside her.

"I was," indifferently replied the woman.

"I'm going to lead a rebellion," conspiratorially whispered Menderchuck. "And I need your clan's help."

Inju paused for a moment, staring Menderchuck up and down.

"No, no," Inju shook her head, returning to her work. "There's only sixteen of us left. That's not near enough."

"It wouldn't just be you," eagerly explained Menderchuck. "I've already got the Zetti to join me."

"Phfff," condescended Inju. "The Zetti? Really? What's that, eight people, nine at most?"

"At least nine and a half," responded Menderchuck. "Sven got better. Hey Sven!... well, sorta better."

Menderchuck waved over toward Sven, who stood thirty feet away. Sven wore a massive bruise upon his head and lurched awkwardly as he moved. With a great smile on only half of his face, he happily waved back.

"Definitely no," replied Inju with an air of finality.

"What are you doing, you idiot!!" screamed out a furious voice far behind them.

As one, Inju and Menderchuck glanced back

over their shoulders, down the line of wheat sheaves which lay upon the ground, past the boy, to a distant slave who was approaching an old wooden wagon that was piled high with wheat.

"Hurry up!" rudely commanded the voice.

It was then that voice's owner came into view. Riding upon his black stallion, a furious foreman Collins approached the distant slave. Terrified, the slave bent down and wrapped his hands around a sheaf of wheat. As he rose to his feet, the wheat sheaf unraveled, raining wheat stalks upon the ground.

"No, no, no!" cried out the foreman, pulling his iron truncheon from his belt.

CRACK With one rage filled swing, foreman Collins brutally brought his iron truncheon down upon the slave's head, splitting it open for all to see. Limply, the slave's body collapsed to the ground.

"You," firmly commanded the foreman to a nearby slave. "Take his place."

Anxiously, the new slave scurried to the line of wheat sheaves. Eyes wide with fear, he bent down, wrapping his hands around a wheat sheaf. To his horror, as the rose to his feet, the sheaf of wheat unraveled in his very hands.

"It's not my fault, master," pleaded the slave, raising his hands to protect his face.

But foreman Collins took little notice. His sharp beady eyes had already found another target.

"Move," grunted the foreman, fiercely jabbing his boots' metal spurs into his horse's fleshy sides.

The horse bolted forward, swiftly carrying its rider toward the young work boy who was hunched over, busily tying sheaves of wheat. The black stallion let out a disgruntled snort as the foreman roughly yanked back on the reigns, bringing the horse to an abrupt stop beside the boy. With fury in his eyes, foreman Collins glared down at the poor boy.

"Boy!" erupted the foreman. "Do you know that we're on a strict schedule, set by the Duke himself?"

"Y... yes.." fearfully stammered the child, looking up at the man who towered above him.

"Boy, stand when you address me," interrupted foreman Collins.

With a wary eye upon the foreman's iron truncheon, the boy timidly rose to his feet.

"Y... yes..."

"Shut up, stupid," declared the foreman, once again cutting off the boy's words.

It was then that foreman Collins noticed the boy's fearful gaze.

"Are you scared of this?" taunted the foreman,

lifting his bloody truncheon before him.

Body shaking, the boy said not a word, but silently nodded his head.

"Well you shouldn't be," declared the foreman, placing the truncheon back into his belt. "You should be scared of this."

Foreman Collins' knuckles turned white as he grasped his sword's ivory hilt and pulled it from his scabbard.

"Now," demanded foreman Collins, lifting his blade slowly toward the boy's throat. "Did you tie all these sheaves yourself?"

"I tied them! It's my fault," cried out a voice.

Surprised, both the boy and the foreman turned toward the voice. There they saw Menderchuck rushing towards them.

"It's my fault master. It's all my fault," lied Menderchuck, covering for the boy. "Nobody taught me this stuff. I just know horse riding."

"Oh, you're saying you're too useless to know how to tie sheaves?" asked the foreman, his voice laced heavy with threat.

"Not exactly, master. As my mother used to say, I'm a bit dense," lied Menderchuck. "My daddy often accused her of throwing away the baby and keeping the afterbirth."

"Really?" smirked the foreman.

"Yes, master," groveled Menderchuck. "Now if someone as masterful as yourself could teach me how to tie properly, well, I'd be ever so grateful, and I promise sir, I'll be the best tie-r you ever did see. I never wanted to hold up harvest. I'm so sorry."

"Yes, you are sorry," agreed foreman Collins with an air of superiority.

Silently sitting high upon his steed, foreman Collins looked down upon Menderchuck and the boy. With a twist of his body, the foreman turned his back to both slaves, dismounting his horse. Trembling, the young boy balled his hands into resolute fists.

"No," silently mouthed Menderchuck. "Go."

Menderchuck waved the boy up the wheat line towards Inju. The boy hesitated for a second, then rushed along the wheat field. The foreman's spurs jingled softly as his boots met the ground, turning to face Menderchuck.

"What is he doing?" asked the foreman, watching the boy rush into the distant Inju's arms.

"Well," suggested Menderchuck. "You probably scared the piss out of him."

A cruel smile crossed the foreman's face, joyful at the thought of scaring the young boy.

"First," explained the foreman, pointing his sword toward one of the wheat sheaves that the

132

boy had already tied. "You need to get down to the level of the cut wheat."

With stiff knees, Menderchuck began to bend down towards the ground. Suddenly a burst of pain erupted from his kidneys as foreman Collins slammed the hilt of his sword to Menderchuck's back.

"UGGGHFFFF!" wheezed Menderchuck, collapsing onto the wheat sheaf.

Menderchuck's eyes watered. His chest heaved in short desperate breathes, laying sprawled out upon the wheat. Then he felt the hard leather soul of the foreman's boot pressing down upon his neck, pinning him helplessly to the ground.

"Get a good long look at that horrible knot tying job," declared foreman Collins, lifting his sword above Menderchuck. "This is your lesson."

"Oawwggghh," painfully gasped Menderchuck, as he felt the sharp metallic sting of the foreman's sword pierce his left arm.

"I don't like being behind schedule," firmly declared the foreman, twisting the sword tip slightly in Menderchuck's arm.

"I THINK I'D LIKE A DAY OFF!" shouted out a distant voice.

Instantly, Menderchuck recognized the voice as Sven's.

"I think we all deserve a day off!" reiterated Sven

in a distracting voice that carried far and wide. "Why don't we all just put down our tools and enjoy a nice day off?"

A look of frustration washed over the foreman's face while he glanced across the field towards Sven, who was pacing frantically around.

"Some one take care of him!" yelled out foreman Collins.

Whips in hand, a few other guards began to ride towards Sven.

"In fact," shouted out Sven, sneaking a peak over towards the foreman. "I think we all deserve a raise! What are we making now, nothing? I think we should get at least twice that!"

"Ugh," grunted foreman Collins, pulling the sword from Menderchuck's arm.

As two guards on horseback began to approach Sven, foreman Collins lifted his boot from Menderchuck's neck. Impatiently, the foreman rushed to his stallion, deftly mounting the beast, and spurring it toward Sven.

As the crack of whips and Sven's pain filled screams crossed the plantation grounds, Menderchuck slowly sat up, placing a tender hand upon his wounded arm. Small rivulets of crimson blood flowed from the wound and over his fingers.

"Let me take care of that," whispered the

comforting voice of Inju.

Menderchuck looked up, surprised to see Inju before him. Gently, she pulled the cloth from her hair and tied it around Menderchuck's arm, binding the wound and staunching the flow of blood.

"Clan Oghul is with you," whispered Inju with a firm nod of the head.

CHAPTER 20: THE NIGHT WIND

As the cool kiss of the night's wind brushed along Torfulson's skin, and the love serenades of a chorus of amorous crickets graced his ears; Torfulson gazed up into the expansive night sky above, watching the twinkling glow of the distant stars that made up the great constellation Arabeth.

"You see that bright one over there," instructed Glenn, pointing eastward. "That's the north star."

Both men, wearing the purple uniforms of their trade upon their bodies and swords upon their sides, diligently stood night guard upon the far edges of the Westernson plantation within sight of the forlorn slave quarters.

"Actually," corrected Torfulson. "That's Kreltor the deceiver. If you look over there, the stars that make up the arrow of Methos' bow, they point to the north star."

"Wow Torfy, you sure know a lot about stars."

Torfulson smiled quietly to himself.

"What's that?!" whispered Glenn in an excited tone, pointing to the west.

Slowly, Torfulson's eyes followed the imaginary line drawn by Glenn's finger, half expecting to find another constellation in need of identification. To Torfulson's surprise, his eyes were met instead with the dark silhouetted visage of a man astride a horse, who stood but a long stone's throw away.

"See!" urgently whispered Glenn. "It's Menderchuck the barbarian king. I told you all I saw him! I told you!"

Silently, Torfulson watched the distant silhouette with curiosity, knowing full well that Menderchuck was fast asleep in the slave quarters behind them.

"We.. we... we gotta go to the plantation house and report this!" whispered Glenn, tugging on Torfulson's arm.

"Why don't you go report this?" suggested Torfulson, eyes transfixed upon the dark figure. "I'll stay here and keep an eye on him."

"Good idea," blurted Glenn, darting off like a spooked pheasant in the direction of the far off plantation house.

Torfulson, though, took little notice of his fleeing compatriot. Instead, his inquisitive stare remained steadfastly fixed upon the distant mysterious stranger. The dark silhouette stood there motionless upon his horse as though waiting for something or someone.

In an earlier life, Torfulson would have fearfully followed Glenn, but now curiosity gripped his soul. Wasting little time, Torfulson ducked down into the tall grass which surrounded him. With a good measure of trepidation, he began to creep below the grass line towards the mysterious figure in search of a better view.

To Torfulson's worried ears, each blade of grass that brushed against his crawling body sounded as though it was amplified a thousand times. Yet cautiously, awkward crawling shuffle by awkward crawling shuffle, he pressed on, tacking towards a lone bush which stood but twenty feet away from the dark rider.

No sooner had Torfulson reached the bush, when he popped up into a crouch, hiding behind the leafy shrub. Timidly, he peeped around the bush, trying in vain to identify the mysterious silhouette. Suddenly, a lump of fear leaped into Torfulson's throat as both beast and rider turned in his direction.

With all the grace of a freshly made sandwich falling upon the floor, Torfulson dropped to the ground. Eyes wide with panic, he discovered a gap in the base of bush's leafy foliage before him. Quickly, like a rabbit escaping a wolf, he scurried into the bush. Though the bush's internal branches harassed him, poking into his sides, he sat there silently as the night wind lightly teased the bush's leaves around him.

"Please don't come this way, please don't come this way," desperately prayed Torfulson under his breath.

His prayers, though, went unheard. To his horror, he distinctly heard the sounds of hoof steps approaching. Closer and closer they neared, until they finally stopped beside the bush.

For a moment, all was quiet. But the quiet was soon replace by ominous sounds of scraping branches, as a creature began to slowly push its head into the bush. Fearfully, Torfulson's right hand drifted down towards the white bone handle knife which hung upon his belt. As he silently wrapped his fingers around the knife's handle, the creature's head erupted through leaves, coming face to face with Torfulson.

"Muffin!" joyfully cried Torfulson, arms caught in the branches as he tried in vain to hug his loyal steed.

Muffin playfully nuzzled him in joyous reunion.

"Torfulson?" came the rider's perplexed voice, which sounded a lot like Pavel.

Torfulson awkwardly stood up, branches latching on to him, forcing his way out of the bush.

"Pavel!" erupted Torfulson.

Pavel leapt from the donkey's back.

"It is good to see you!" exclaimed Pavel, hugging Torfulson in greeting. "I've been looking for you and Menderchuck, everywhere."

"You found me," smiled Torfulson.

"I've got great news. Muffin and I have been riding by night, scouting around. I've located the rest of the clan. They're spread across three different plantations to the north, east and south of here."

"That must have taken forever to find."

"Not really," explained Pavel. "The plantations are all lined up like dots on a giant circle. Once I figured that out, it was easy to figure out where the next one, and the next one, and the next one would be located. The tough part was finding the ones with our people. But that didn't turn out too hard either, the other horse riders..."

"The slaves?"

"Yeah, they hid me, and fed me in each plantation that I came to..." Pavel interrupted his own train of thought. "But I'm wasting time with stories. There will be time for that later. Grab Menderchuck, I can lead us to the plantations which hold our people."

"Umm... about that..." stuttered Torfulson. "Menderchuck doesn't want to do that. He refuses to abandon the people here. He wants to start the rebellion here."

"Alright...," sighed Pavel, thinking for a moment. "That wouldn't have been my call, but if that's the Chief's decree, then so be it. He knows best. How's the rebellion here going? You and Menderchuck ready to strike?"

Frustratedly, Torfulson kicked the grass around his feet, "Ummm... not exactly.... but we're working on it."

"Excellent, so what should I do in the meantime?"

"Ummm..." Torfulson thought out loud. "My dad would probably tell you to do something foolhardy, like stab everyone you see. But it's probably better if you keep making connections at the plantations, so that if we succeed here, they'll be ready for us."

Pavel nodded in agreement as Muffin nuzzled Torfulson for pats.

CLANG *CLANG* *CLANG*

The plantation's distant alarm bell cried out, destroying the peace of night.

"Go quickly," instructed Torfulson. "I'll send them off in the wrong direction. Oh, and keep him safe."

"I will," reassured Pavel, mounting the donkey.

"I was talking to Muffin."

CHAPTER 21: A BUSY MORNING

Duke Belloch sat alone in his great leather chair behind his mighty oak desk in his grand fifth floor office. Even by his standards, his morning had been overwhelmingly busy, dealing with the reports of a dozen plus plantations.

"A fledgling empire does not run itself," he consoled himself as he finally put the last report to bed.

Though the Duke would have been loath to admit it, things had been a bit busier since he had sent Oleg off days ago in pursuit of the horse merchant Evander.

With a heavy head and even heavier eyelids, Duke Belloch leaned back into his chair, resting his eyes. Like a fallen leaf riding upon the surface of a flowing river, the Duke soon drifted away to the land of dreams.

There he beheld a sight that even made his sleeping self smile. His dream self stood upon the greater outer balcony of St. Ufstath's cathedral as the refreshing breeze of a balmy summer's day blew through his hair. Confidently, he strode to the balcony's edge where he was greeted by the joyous cheers of a great multitude.

Below the Steppes' great clear blue sky, filling every street, alley, and park in the city, there stood immense crowds of loyal subjects, all who looked up at Duke Belloch with reverence and awe. And beyond them, standing in formation upon all four roads that lead to Siztok, reaching to the horizon in all directions, there stood a great army, the army of Belloch.

"My loyal subjects!" declared the Duke from the balcony to the great masses below. "This is the dawn of a new order. None shall stand against us!"

A joyous cheer erupted from the crowd. But then, in the briefest of heart beats, the joyous cheers turned into terrified screams. The bright shining sun darkened, and the clear blue sky turned an ominous red.

As the masses below fled in terror, Duke Belloch desperately scanned the horizon for the cause of this turn in fortune, and then he saw it.

In the south, a great multitude of horse raiders, led by the ferocious barbarian king Menderchuck, emerged from the ground itself. Their numbers blotted out the land like a great swarm of locusts. They rode like lightning with their blood curdling war cries flying in advance, announcing their dreaded approach. Like a great tidal wave, they effortlessly smashed through the Duke's army before them in a deadly collision course with Siztok itself.

"Close the gates! Close the gates!" screamed out Duke Belloch.

And the order was given not a moment too soon. Siztok's massive gates closed tight only moments before the barbarian horde reached the town's great moat.

"Ohwufff," exclaimed the Duke, letting out a long sigh of relief.

But his relief was short lived. To the Duke's horror, the barbarians' mounts drank the moat dry, then they began to cross the barren moat bed. As the barbarian horde climbed out of the moat, approaching Siztok's great defenses, the city's walls turned to sand, blowing away in the wind.

"Nooo!" impotently screamed out Duke Belloch.

Great plumes of smoke rose up from the city below as the barbarian horde sacked Siztok. Then the horde turned as one towards St. Ufstath's cathedral in search of Duke Belloch himself.

This same nightmare had tormented the Duke's dreams every night since he had received Glenn's letter, but it was here that the dreams would weirdly diverge. One night, Menderchuck captured the Duke, saddled him, and rode him about like a horse playing polo. Another night, the Duke dreamed that he had turned into a bird, flying safely away from the horde, only to return to his bird family and discover that his wife was an angry old crow. She cawed furiously at him for not returning with something shiny. Last night, the dream had ended with him and Menderchuck working together in a lemonade stand. They were busy with customers, but they were all out of lemons. The Duke looked in vain for more, lest he would be fired, but could find none.

SLAM The doors of Duke Belloch's office burst open, awakening the Duke and rescuing him from his nightmare. Nostrils flaring while huffy breathes escaped his startled lungs, the Duke's wide eyes glanced about in search of the sound's origin.

There, in the doors' open frame, stood Oleg. Roughly, he dragged the chained body of Evander, the horse merchant, behind him. Oleg wore a beaming smile upon his face which revealed his yellowed teeth and a large silly hat upon his head. The hat was made of leather with a wide brim that was covered in garnets. The crown of the hat stood three feet tall, like a small chimney, and was adorned in a plethora of brightly colored feathers. With each step that Oleg took, the hat would sway wildly from side to side. Upon Oleg's chest, he wore a golden chain that held the gold seal of the city which was warped and bent.

Duke Belloch frowned disapprovingly as he looked upon Oleg, "What in the world are you wearing?"

"Oh, it's my new Lord Mayor Hat," proudly crowed Oleg. "Looks pretty professional, doesn't it?"

"No...., why are you wearing a bent seal of Siztok?"

"Remember how the old Lord Mayor fell to his death?"

Duke Belloch nodded silently as Evander watched on in confusion.

"Well," continued Oleg. "His fat self fell on the seal and bent it. I've been trying to bend it back, but I just end up making it worse."

"I see..."

"Oh, you should have been there today," excitedly interrupted Oleg. "It was a great ceremony!"

"What ceremony?"

"You forgot? Remember when we drowned all those peasants in the moat?" asked Lord Mayor Oleg.

"How could I forget?" complained the Duke. "I could hear their wailing from here. It was most annoying."

"Today was the ceremony to celebrate... I mean honor the dead of the so called accident," eagerly explained Oleg. "I got to pull a rope, and it dropped a tarp, revealing a statue in their honor. There were crying widows and children, it was great fun."

The Duke glared daggers at Oleg.

"Right boss! Sorry boss! To the business at hand," declared Oleg roughly yanking on Evander's chains, pulling him forward.

The right side of Evander's face was thoroughly

bruised as though he had been hit repeatedly.

"Tell him what you told me, go on," commanded Oleg, rudely jabbing Evander in the ribs.

"I think Oleg's hat looks like it's taking a poo, and Oleg is its turd," grinned Evander.

SMACK

Oleg's fist collided with the side of Evander's head.

"Owww!" exclaimed the horse merchant in pain. "No one can take constructive criticism these days."

"When it comes to the hat, we are in agreement, merchant," coolly proclaimed the Duke. "But that is not why I invited you here."

"If this is your idea of an invitation," quipped Evander, ratting the chains that bound him. "I'd hate to see what happens when you bring someone here forcefully."

Unimpressed, Duke Belloch folded his arms.

"Righto, down to business," coughed Evander. "As I told your loutish friend here, yes, I've seen Menderchuck, sometime back."

"How many were there?" impatiently demanded the Duke.

"There's just one Menderchuck. It's not like

there's a group of Menderchuck's walking around. That'd be weird."

"Don't toy with me!" snapped Duke Belloch before quickly recovering his composure.

"He was alone," lied Evander, who knew full well that a good sales pitch had just enough truth to seem credible, but not so much truth as to ruin the sale. "It was just him. I sold him my last horse, a decrepit old mare. You took everything else from me. It was all I had left. Sigh... I even took a loss on that sale. Only got two gold, we needed the money for food..."

Duke Belloch turned towards Oleg, "What was his ranch like when you got there?"

"Empty, like we left it. Not a horse to be found. Looks like business is bad," snickered Oleg.

"Whooo!" exclaimed Duke Belloch, letting out a sigh of relief. "That is the best news that I've heard all day. I'm feeling better already."

"But that means Menderchuck is alive and out there," warily whispered Oleg.

"Yes, yes, who cares," dismissively answered the Duke. "We've already put down a slave rebellion or three on the plantations. One more barbarian is no big deal. It's only a problem if he's already assembled a horse army, and he's not. Our system can easily handle a rogue barbarian or an isolated rebellion."

The troubled look on Oleg's face said that he

wasn't quite so sure.

"You're just scared that he's going to kill you for revenge," consoled the Duke. "And, for what it's worth, if I was him, I'd try to kill you too, but use your logical brain. One barbarian can't take on our army. Trust in my system. It hasn't let us down yet."

Oleg did not find the words particularly reassuring. The Duke, though, looked lighter than he had in days, almost preening as he leapt up and walked around his desk.

"Put out a reward for Menderchuck," commanded Duke Belloch. "One hundred gold for any guard that brings him in, and twenty gold for any slave that reveals his location."

Oleg's face remained stoic as he replied, "They won't turn on him."

"Why not?" smiled the Duke. "You did for gold and slaves."

Oleg stood there speechlessly. Sometimes the truth stings.

"Now," instructed Duke Belloch. "Show our friend Evander here out."

"Out the balcony?" inquired Oleg.

"No, no, no," explained the Duke with a relieved smile. "Just unchain him and let him go. Helpful subservient people should always be rewarded. We're not barbarians here."

CHAPTER 22: HUNGER

"No," scoffed Golgoth, holding his empty bowl before him.

Overwhelmed by frustration, Menderchuck kicked the dirt beneath him. In the growing shadows of late dusk beside the slave quarters' decrepit shacks, both men stood at the head of a long snaking line of famished slaves. For the better part of an hour, the two men, wooden bowls in hand, had patiently worked their way to the front of the line.

A kitchen slave, wearing a soiled apron, wearily dipped her ladle into the large bucket which rested upon the rustic table before her. A thick clump of cold lumpy gruel stuck to the ladle as she lifted it from the bucket, then dumped it into Golgoth's bowl. Golgoth the giant gave the kitchen slave a thankful nod, then turned to leave.

Impatiently, Menderchuck held out his bowl to the kitchen slave, keenly watching Golgoth walk away. The moment that Menderchuck heard the wet plop of cold gruel land in his bowl, he turned and scurried off after Golgoth.

"Come on, come on," pressured Menderchuck for the hundredth time. "I've got the Oghul and the Zetti. They're in, but we need more. If you join us, I bet the rest fall in line."

"What did I say the other times you asked me?"

"We need you and your men," pleaded Menderchuck. "Our rebellion won't succeed without you."

Golgoth stopped dead in his tracks, coldly staring down into Menderchuck's eyes.

"You wouldn't even succeed with us," replied Golgoth with a heavy heart. "Enough of us have died already. The age of the horse clans is over. The answer is no, now and forever. Now leave me be, old man."

Golgoth turned his back to Menderchuck and walked off. Weeks of futile frustration boiled over in Menderchuck's psyche.

"OH, PISSY BOTTOMS!" erupted Menderchuck, hurling his bowl to the ground.

His regret was instant. The bowl collided hard with the ground below, liberally spraying out its contents.

"Aaahhh, noooooo," groaned Menderchuck, hungrily looking down at his supper which now lay spilled across the ground.

Forlornly, he glanced back towards the rustic food table and its long snaking line. Then, with a defeated sigh, he bent to his knees and began to scrape what gruel he could back into his bowl. When he had finished scraping, he rose to his feet, disappointedly looking down into his bowl of gruel that was now garnished with bits of dirt and grass.

It was then that he heard the faint sound of music drifting on the wind. Menderchuck's hungry eyes rose up from his bowl, staring across the field toward the distant great plantation house. The sound of a string quartet emanated from the mansion's brightly lit open windows which shone like a lighthouse against the ever darkening evening sky.

"Somewhere in there," jealousy thought Menderchuck. "Torf is enjoying a big steak."

Menderchuck was wrong. They were having roast pheasant.

As a despondent melancholy washed over Menderchuck, a wayward fly landed on the edge of his bowl, then slipped and fell into the gruel below. Menderchuck watched intently as the fly struggled to pull itself out of the lumpy grey slop. But the more it struggled to be free, the more it sank down toward its gruelly fate.

Menderchuck raised his free hand up, then dipped his index finger into the gruel. In one motion, he scooped out the desperate fly. Slowly he lifted both finger and fly towards his mouth. He watched for a second as the small creature struggled with the gruel that still coated its wings. Menderchuck gently pursed his lips, blowing lightly upon the fly and dislodging the gruel's remains. The fly then stretched its wings and leapt off of his finger, flying away.

"Be free, friend," whispered Menderchuck, intently watching the fly disappear into the dark of evening.

Perhaps in that moment, Menderchuck saw a bit of himself in that fly. Or perhaps, he was just too stupid to give up. Either way, a small spark lit the pilot light of desperate hope. Menderchuck looked towards a group of fellow slaves who were huddled together on rough hewn benches around the flicking glow of a nearby campfire. Bowl in hand, he strode boldly towards them.

"You know what tastes better than this delicious gruel?" confidently began Menderchuck, eating a big spoonful of gruel.

As the gruel touched his tongue, his face scrunched up in a grimace.

"Uhhggghh, most everything," he muttered to himself.

To his great surprise, this got a weak laugh from his fellow horse riders. Menderchuck smiled, maybe this was a start.

"It's not right that those in the big house eat steak, while we eat this."

Menderchuck gestured to his bowl of gruel while some of the slaves around him nodded in agreement.

"We do all the work! We deserve the steak!" boldly declared Menderchuck to noticeable agreement. "And you know what tastes even better than steak?!"

The small crowd of once proud horse riders turned destitute slaves watched him in curious anticipation to discover what was better than steak.

"FREEDOM!" shouted Menderchuck. "We should all be free. First we must....."

The moment he cried out the word "freedom," his fellow slaves began to stand up and quickly shuffle away. Forlornly, Menderchuck watched them go, then he reluctantly sat down upon one of the many now vacated rough hewn benches.

"Huhhhh," dejectedly sighed Menderchuck from the depths of his soul, finding himself alone beside the crackling campfire.

Despondently, he looked down into his bowl of gruel as the quiet night sounds of crickets chirping and the murmur of distant slaves chatting swirled around him. Suddenly, the peaceful sounds of evening were obliterated by the din of a charging horse and its rider.

"Hear me, hear me!" cried out Glenn the guard astride his mighty steed, bursting into the slave camp.

The voices of slaves fell quiet as all eyes turned toward Glenn.

"By order of Duke Belloch himself!" loudly proclaimed Glenn. "Menderchuck the barbarian has been spotted skulking by night like a coward. Worry not, we shall protect you from his vile deeds!"

Judging by the silence that met the guard's

words, the slaves were not particularly worried about Menderchuck and his "vile deeds."

"Any who are discovered to be in collabra... collebre... collybration... working with Menderchuck will be put to the sword!" threatened Glenn as he literally rattled his sword. "Any who reveal the location of Menderchuck, will be rewarded with twenty whole gold guilders to use as you please! Now, who has seen him?!"

Acutely aware of his exposed position alone by a fire, Menderchuck slunk his shoulders, wishing that he could disappear. His anxious eyes darted around in desperate glances at his fellow distant slaves, fearing that he might be exposed at any moment.

"Well?!" loudly demanded Glenn, who secretly wanted to claim the reward for himself.

The sounds of crickets in the night were his only response.

"You, loser who sits alone!" cried out Glenn, pointing towards Menderchuck. "Think of all you could buy with twenty gold guilders. Maybe you could afford some friends! The gold could be yours, now where is Menderchuck?"

"I, I don't know," lied Menderchuck as a tingle of fear crept up his spine.

The guard's nostrils flared with an angry grunt. Slowly, he stared down the many groups of slaves who rested around adjacent campfires.

"One of you morons must know! Where is Menderchuck?!" demanded Glenn.

The quiet cowered stares of a hundred plus slaves were his only reply.

"Fine!" angrily screamed out Glenn. "You're all a bunch of stinky poo heads, and I hate you all! I'll go find him myself!"

And with that, Glenn the guard spurred his horse into a gallop, charging away from the slave quarters and into the fields beyond.

As fear was replaced by relief, Menderchuck let out a long slow sigh, like a deflating balloon. Once again, the quiet murmur of conversations, the chirping of crickets, the crackling of campfires, and the distant wispy sounds of string music emanating from the great plantation house across the field retook their rightful places in the symphony of the night.

Menderchuck gazed down into his bowl of gruel. Though his eyes said "no," his stomach screamed out "yes, now!" Real hunger has a way of changing one's perspective. Greedily, he dipped his spoon into the bowl, pulling out a great spoonful of gruel which he voraciously shoved into his mouth.

In that moment, to Menderchuck's surprise, a man sat down beside him upon the rough hewn bench. Though the man was a fellow slave, his clothes were nicer, and he was much better fed than most. For some reason that Menderchuck did not yet understand, the man had chosen to sit uncomfortably close to him.

"Herphhh," said Menderchuck with his spoon still in his mouth, before hastily removing it. "Hi."

At first, the man said nothing. Instead, he looked Menderchuck up and down for an awkward moment. Then he opened his mouth.

"I'm Xerc."

"Hi Xerc, I'm..." Menderchuck instantly cut himself off, changing subjects. "I'm enjoying the music coming from the plantation house. How about you?"

"Could I have your bowl of gruel?" asked Xerc, ignoring Menderchuck's words.

Menderchuck smiled jovially, "I know it might be hard to believe, but I'm not finished with it yet. Even if eating it is, grueling."

Menderchuck laughed very loudly at his awful pun while Xerc sat in stony silence.

Then a note of menace snuck into Xerc's voice, "I don't think you understand me, Menderchuck."

Menderchuck's blood turned ice cold at the sound of his own name.

"Look around, you have few friends here," said Xerc, gesturing with his hand. "And I doubt any of them are willing to die for you."

Menderchuck did look around. About thirty feet away, he saw a group of slaves standing conspiratorially together. In the center of the group was Golgoth the giant and his friend Enok. Both Golgoth and Enok glared back in Menderchuck's direction.

"We too once rode the plains. We all know the great Menderchuck," observed Xerc, his voice dripping with sarcasm. "Well...., maybe not all of us. The guards might like to know that the man they seek is under their very noses. The Duke would be very pleased with them for capturing you."

Xerc gently reached out his hand, "Now you were saying something about wanting to give me that bowl of food."

Menderchuck was not the fastest horse in the stable, but he very much understood what Xerc was saying. Reluctantly, he placed his bowl of gruel into the creepy man's hands.

"That's much better," dismissively declared Xerc, standing up.

Xerc pulled a spoonful of gruel out of the bowl and looked down at Menderchuck.

"I think you understand the arrangement. From now on, if I'm hungry, your food is mine," Xerc stated with an air of superiority. "Oh, and I will be wanting other things in the future too."

"But... I'll die without food," helplessly protested Menderchuck.

"You'll die if Duke Belloch finds you here," coldly threatened Xerc.

Then, with a prideful smile, Xerc gulped down the spoonful of gruel and walked off as Menderchuck's hungry eyes longingly followed his former bowl.

CHAPTER 23: BEDTIME

It was a dark, hot, smelly night inside of the overcrowded slave shack. A sliver of moonlight snuck in through the shack's glassless windows, barely illuminating the great mass of sleeping bodies that covered the long room's dirt floor. Menderchuck too lay on the floor, but he was not asleep. He lay with one eye open, waiting.

"Xerc must die," he thought to himself.

Xerc was a threat. He knew Menderchuck's identity and had threatened to expose him.

"No witnesses. I just need to get him alone," Menderchuck's thoughts raced while his hungry stomach rumbled.

Menderchuck's logical mind knew for a fact that one of the numerous bodies, which slumbered in the dark around him, was Xerc. Like a tiger stalking a gazelle, Menderchuck had cautiously trailed his extorter ever since their encounter, eventually leading here.

"If he's even in here..." whispered Menderchuck's doubt. "I saw him enter the shack, but not where he lay. Did he sneak out in the dark? No, he couldn't. I've watched the door this whole time. Or could he have?.."

In the dark of the night, time moves slowly, and anxious thoughts advance quickly, assaulting even the strongest citadels of logic. As the hours crept by and the nightly lullaby of crickets sang the world to sleep, Menderchuck's eyelids began to droop, bearing the exhaustion of a long workday slaving away in the fields. Anxiety, though, is a bitch goddess, giving with one hand and taking away with the other. While his tired body demanded sleep, his anxious mind refused it.

It was then, when things felt bleakest, that Menderchuck heard a small grunt far behind him. Slowly, silently, tensely, he rolled over to face toward the sound. There, in the back of the room, a dark silhouette rose to its feet. Cautiously, it snaked through the sleeping multitude. Its feet methodically searched for the few unoccupied spaces of dirt floor between sleeping slaves while heading in Menderchuck's direction. As the silhouette passed by the window, the side of his face was revealed in the pale moonlight.

"Xerc!" thought Menderchuck, suddenly closing his eyes, feigning sleep.

Like a hidden rabbit desperately listening for any sound of the wolf, Menderchuck's ears strained to capture Xerc's every movement. *thud* *thud* *thud* Quietly rang out the sounds of Xerc's deliberate approaching footsteps, as he carefully worked his way through the mass of sleeping bodies. Closer and closer, the sound of Xerc's footsteps came, pausing right beside Menderchuck's laying body.

In that briefest of moments, Menderchuck held his anxious breath, waiting for what would come next. *thud* Came the sound of Xerc's foot as he stepped over Menderchuck, who let out a silent sigh of relief. Quiet as a church mouse, Menderchuck slightly cracked open his eyelids and turned his head, watching a hazy Xerc walking away on his path to the shack's main exit. No sooner had Xerc disappeared out of the front door, when Menderchuck tensed his muscles in preparation to leap up in pursuit.

"Pssp.. psssp... pssssp," whispered out two conspiratorial voices.

Menderchuck froze, startled heart furiously beating. As he gazed across the dark room toward the sound, he beheld two new dark silhouettes rising from the floor, one much taller than the other.

"Golgoth? Enok?" worriedly realized Menderchuck.

As silently as Xerc before them, the giant and his companion carefully made their way through the mass of sleeping slaves to the front door, disappearing out of the shack.

"So, it's a good ol' fashioned midnight poop party, is it?" whispered Menderchuck to himself, leaping up to his feet in stealthy pursuit.

CHAPTER 24: XERC

As a young child on the plains, Menderchuck had learned to move silently while stalking his prey. And in the same way, he now trailed the three men out into the hot night air.

Xerc hurried north towards the moonlit main thoroughfare that led into the plantation grounds. Once there, he wasted little time, turning his back to the plantation. And so the odd procession moved quickly up the road, leaving the plantation grounds behind with Xerc in the lead, Golgoth and Enok following some twenty feet behind, and Menderchuck secretly bringing up the distant rear.

"How... how am I going to do this?" frantically whispered Menderchuck to himself. "I need to get Xerc alone."

A small dark forest composed of elder trees, whose memories were as long as their deep seated roots, rested north of the road just beyond the plantation's boundaries. A minor flowing river snaked through the forest, emerging out its south side, intersecting with the road at the foot of a wooden bridge. It was there, just before the bridge on the edge of the forest, that Xerc stopped cold in his tracks. For a moment, he just stood there, then he darted into the dark woods.

With inquisitive eyes and a curious heart, Menderchuck looked up the road, watching Golgoth and Enok follow suit, disappearing into the exact same section of the woods.

"No... no... no..." whispered Menderchuck, rapidly picking up his pace.

Menderchuck rushed to the spot of the three men's disappearance. There he stood, staring in vain into the impenetrably dark woods in search of any trace of the three men.

"No, no, no, where are they?!" gasped Menderchuck, running a frantic hand through his hair.

Then Menderchuck too plunged himself into the dark forest.

Perhaps, if Menderchuck had had a candle or an intimate knowledge of the woods, he would have discovered the narrow well worn animal path that worked its way through the forest's heart, but he was not so lucky. Blindly, he stumbled through the pitch black woods, heart leaping in the fear of being discovered as twigs snapped loudly beneath his feet.

There's something about night that seems to amplify sounds. Perhaps it's the relative quiet or perhaps a trick of the night gods. Anyone who has ever tried to sneak home in the middle of the night can testify to such a phenomenon, and these dark woods were no exception.

"Alright, you bastards," whispered Menderchuck, stopping dead in his tracks, ears straining desperately for any sound of the men that he pursued. "Where are you?"

craaack Responded the faint echoing sound of

a branch breaking deep inside of the woods.

"Gotcha!" gasped Menderchuck, breaking into a run.

Now the thing about running in a pitch black forest in the middle of the night is, well, you shouldn't do it. Desperately afraid of losing his escaping quarry, Menderchuck's legs pumped furiously. His body bound through the dark woods, flying five feet, then ten feet, then fifteen feet deeper and deeper into the forest as old gnarled trees whizzed by.

While his body lifted from the ground in mid-stride, his head snapped back violently as his face collided with a thick low hanging tree branch. In one moment, Menderchuck's feet were below him. In the next, his feet were far ahead of him, even with his head as he was violently clotheslined backwards.

THUD

"Ooooffff," painfully gasped Menderchuck, crashing onto his back upon the hard forest floor.

In that second, laying sprawled out upon the cold hard ground, Menderchuck's eyes watered. Perhaps it was caused by the pain of having the wind knocked out of him. Or, perhaps, it was the deeper pain of fighting as hard as you can for a long time and only finding failure.

"Arabeth," frustratedly whispered Menderchuck, his voice dissipating into the dark trees around him. "Please, guide me."

For a moment, the barbarian chief thought that he heard a faint noise well behind him, but it was instantly overshadowed by the far off distant sound of men's voices ahead. Wasting no time, he climbed to his feet.

Carefully this time, awkwardly feeling his way forward, Menderchuck began to follow the trail of voices that floated upon the wind. Though briers and branches resisted him, Menderchuck urgently pushed on. In due time, the trail of sounds led him to the edge of the forest which opened out into the great plains of Rannsaka.

"Wow, it's like the difference between night and night," quietly remarked Menderchuck to himself, gazing out of the dark forest across the vast moonlit grassy plains.

Instantly, Menderchuck's eyes latched onto the source of the voices. There, standing forty feet away in the tall grass, were the three men whom he pursued. Clips and phrases of their heated exchange carried out over the plains.

"Know... truth... reveal... time..."

Cautiously, Menderchuck squatted down behind a bush on the edge of the woods, spying on Xerc, Golgoth, and Enok from afar. Slowly, Menderchuck closed his eyes, focusing on the word snippets that drifted by.

"Enough... Menderchuck... guards....."

At the sound of his own name, Menderchuck's eyelids shot open.

"Aw, crap," sighed Menderchuck. "What do I do? What do I do? I can't possibly take them all on."

The gears of Menderchuck's mind whirled into overdrive, trying to compute an impossible solution that would result in victory against the unassailable giant and his two companions.

It was then, bathed in the pale light of the moon, that the three men's conversation took a sudden turn.

"I'm the one who dic..!" shouted out a furious Xerc, whose words were suddenly choked off by Golgoth's giant hand wrapping firmly around Xerc's neck.

Xerc's eyeballs bulged fearfully with surprise. His mouth gaped opened in protest, but found no air with which to speak. From his hiding place, Menderchuck silently watched as Enok reached behind himself and pulled out a sharpened two foot long stick. Enok then placed the sharpened stick into the giant's free hand. In one brutal swift movement, Golgoth the giant lifted the stick high above his head, then slammed its pointed end deep into Xerc's eye socket.

Even from this range, Menderchuck could see the blood squirt out of Xerc's head, and hear the fatal bone crunching sound of the stick breaking the skull and puncturing Xerc's brain. For a moment, Xerc's body spasmed, before going limp and falling lifelessly to the ground.

As Menderchuck silently watched this all, something brushed against the side of his leg. Instinctively, he jerked around to see what had touched him. Out of the corner of his eye, he saw something green and pointy.

"Gnome hat!" cried out Menderchuck in a high pitched scream, desperately scrambling backwards.

Heart pounding, Menderchuck's scared eyes darted about for any sign of the gnome. A mixture of instant relief and a feeling of stupidity hit him at once as he realized that it wasn't a gnome's hat at all, but a particularly large leaf which hung from the bush. His relief was short lived though, for he heard heavy footsteps approaching his hiding place.

"Crap, crap, craaaap," neurotically whispered Menderchuck, diving into the tall grass before him.

Like a lowly snake surrounded by grass, Menderchuck pressed his body to the ground in hiding, but it was too late. A giant hand reached down and grabbed him as though he were a small boy, effortlessly lifting him up from the ground. There Menderchuck hung, feet dangling in the air, face to face with the giant Golgoth.

"Hiiii..." weakly croaked Menderchuck.

"It figures it'd be you," groaned Golgoth, letting out a long sigh. "You've been nothing, but trouble. That needs to end."

CHAPTER 25: THE CORPSE

In the middle of night, below the vast starry sky, just beyond the small woods on the edge of the Westernson plantation, three men stood around a corpse. Well, actually only two of the men stood in the tall grassy plains. The third, Menderchuck, was held aloft in the grip of Golgoth the giant.

"You need to see this," grunted Golgoth, unceremoniously dropping Menderchuck.

Menderchuck collapsed to the ground, landing face to face with Xerc's corpse. Blood still oozed out of the dead man's eye socket where a thick sharpened stick stuck out of his punctured skull.

"Do you hear something from the woods?" asked Enok.

As Enok and Golgoth distractedly turned their heads to look back at the forest, Menderchuck's mind raced.

"I refuse to die here," determinedly thought Menderchuck.

In a flash, the desperate barbarian scrambled onto to Xerc's corpse. He placed a foot on the corpse's head, and wrapped his hands around the pointed stick. With a fierce pull and a squishing *pop* the stick popped free. Wild eyed, Menderchuck turned towards the two men, waving the pointed stick in front of him.

"Stay away from..." he began.

SLAP Golgoth slapped the pointed stick out of Menderchuck's hand as though he were swatting a fly. It cart wheeled a few revolutions through the air before finally disappearing into the tall grass several feet away.

"STOP!" shouted Golgoth, his rage filled voice echoing out across the empty plains.

The fury of the Golgoth's voice froze Menderchuck in his tracks.

"You are the stupidest most persistent man that I have ever met!"

"Thank you," replied Menderchuck.

"It wasn't a compliment!" bellowed the giant. "You're a complete idiot! Just like your father before you!"

The sharpness of Golgoth's words stabbed deep into Menderchuck's chest. Menderchuck the Terrible could handle being called an idiot, but he could not handle being compared to his father.

"Well... well!" stammered Menderchuck. "You're just a giant stupid head! Look at your freakishly large head, having... having all kinds of stupid thoughts in it!"

The three men stood awkwardly glaring at each other while the tall grass around them flowed in the night breeze.

171

"Are you trying to say?" calmly asked Golgoth. "That because my head is so big, it can hold way more stupid thoughts than a regular man?"

"YES!" exclaimed Menderchuck, clapping his hands together. "That's exactly it! And, and, I'm nothing like my father!"

"You're all the same!" erupted Golgoth, pointing his finger at Menderchuck. "This whole thing, the destruction of the clans, the death of my family, the slavery, it's all your clan's fault!"

"What? How?" protested Menderchuck.

"The elders told us the tales," gravely explained Golgoth as Enok nodded in solemn agreement. "How your clan would enslave innocents, march them through our territory, disrupting our raiding seasons, and sell slaves to the Kingdoms of the West."

"That was my father!" erupted Menderchuck. "Not me. I ended that!"

"It doesn't matter," accused Golgoth. "Your people brought the eyes of the West down upon us, and then your own people betrayed us all."

"Oleg..." sighed Menderchuck with a sudden realization that deflated the angry winds which had filled his sails.

"Oleg," agreed Golgoth with flared nostrils, spitting out the vile word.

For a brief moment, the rustling of the grass in

the wind was the only sound that could be heard as a heavy silence descend upon the three men.

"I told you," defeatedly declared Golgoth, turning toward Enok. "He wouldn't even say thank you."

Menderchuck looked up curiously at the two men.

"It's true," agreed Enok. "He did say that."

"What in the world would I thank you for?!" demanded Menderchuck, throwing his arms up in frustration.

As one, both Golgoth and Enok pointed at Xerc's lifeless body which lay at Menderchuck's feet.

"We suspected he was a collaborator," explained Golgoth, eyes transfixed upon Xerc's plump corpse. "You don't grow fatter as a slave, unless you are. When we saw him take your food that cinched it. He even admitted as much, right before he died."

"Ohhh..." sighed Menderchuck, feeling like a complete fool.

"Ohhh? Ohhhhh?!" Golgoth's words sputtered in his mouth. "OHHHH?! He was going to report you to the guards, but we prevented that! Menderchuck the Terrible? More like, Menderchuck the Ungrateful!"

A cold shiver crossed Menderchuck's body at the

sound of his own name.

"You... you... know who I am?" sheepishly asked Menderchuck.

"Everyone does!" raged Golgoth.

"The guards don't," corrected Enok. "Otherwise he'd be dead."

Enok's reward for the truth was a cold hard glare from Golgoth.

"Sorry, sorry," stumbled Enok. "I get it. Not the right place or time."

"Well..." Menderchuck blurted out defensively. "Maybe you're the ones who should be thanking me!"

"What for?!" frustratedly yelled Golgoth. "For repeatedly attacking me when I did you no wrong?!"

"Yes! No!... Maybe! I... I, I need to take charge, so I can lead us all in a rebellion. So we can be free once again."

"More like get us killed," grumbled the disgruntled giant

"Maybe, the reality is that you're just cowards!" shouted Menderchuck. "Titty babies, who are more than grateful to grovel at master's feet for some milk!"

Golgoth grunted, clenching his fist in rage. As he

did, he felt Enok's calm hand upon his arm, gently restraining him.

"We all lost people in the war," said Enok, the truth of his heavy words pierced the hearts of all around. "Menderchuck, I don't know what you've been doing since the war. How you survived. What you suffered, but us, we have felt the cutting sting of the whip upon our backs. We have born the cold hard steel of the manacle upon our bodies. We've seen rebellions come and go. We have seen the foolish remnants of once proud clans cut down, fighting for a life that is long past. And we have seen the severed heads of rebels, some of them our own kin, paraded from plantation to plantation as a reward for defying Duke Belloch."

Golgoth nodded in solemn agreement.

"Hot heads don't last long here," grimly continued Enok. "And worse, they lead others to their death. It seems so easy, just over power the guards, and you're free."

"That's what I'm saying!" erupted Menderchuck. "What we nee..."

Menderchuck's brash words died in his mouth as Enok calmly continued.

"The thing is," finished Enok. "The guards aren't the main problem. The Duke's army is, and it is always nearby, just out of sight, eagerly waiting to kill us, to torture us, to put us down like animals. We have neither the men nor the arms to fight an army."

CLANG *CLANG* *CLANG* Suddenly rang out the plantation house's distant alarm bell.

"I, I told you I heard something from the woods!" fearfully cried out Enok.

"Psh, don't worry," scoffed Menderchuck. "The plantation house is a ways away. We got time."

"BARUUUU!" howled out a chorus of dogs, echoing out from the nearby woods.

"O... ok...," stuttered Menderchuck. "Maybe worry a little."

"BARRUUUU!" called out the dog pack again, getting closer and closer.

"Everybody run!" commanded Golgoth.

What happened next would change the course of all of their lives.

"No," coldly disputed Menderchuck, eyes fixed upon the dark forest. "We can't out run the dogs. Both of you, go. I got this."

Golgoth and Enok exchanged a quick quiet glance, nodded, then fled deeper into the Steppes. Menderchuck stood alone in the moonlit grassy plains over the corpse of Xerc.

"BARRUUUUU!" threateningly cried out the approaching creatures.

"Please be Torf, please be Torf, please let it be

Torf that finds me," panickly whispered Menderchuck.

Five vicious hunting hounds charged through the bushes on the forest's edge, emerging into the moonlit plains. Their leashes were taught, pulling a guard behind them. It was not Torfulson.

"Ohh, Horse poo!" spat out an angry and scared Menderchuck.

CHAPTER 26: THE GUARD

With white knuckled hands, the guard desperately clung to the five leather leashes which were attached to the hunting hounds' spiked collars. Barking viciously, the dogs forcefully dragged the guard out of the dark woods and into the moonlit grassy plains. It was then that the guard's eyes met Menderchuck's.

"Oh boy," gasped Menderchuck, fearfully watching the guard and hounds who stood only forty feet away. "I'll never out run them. I, I need... I need to get rid of the dogs."

As he looked across the meadow toward the guard, a look of recognition came over Menderchuck's face.

"Glenn!" whispered Menderchuck, desperately wracking his brain for useful information. "What did Torf tell me about Glenn? He's allergic to sheep? No, that's not it. He has an annoying habit of kicking the table? No, that's Adam, and that's useless anyways."

"BARRRRUUUU" howled the dogs, pulling Glenn the guard in Menderchuck's direction.

"Ugh, stupid Torf with all his complaining about the other guards!" gasped Menderchuck, kicking the grass around him. "What a cry baby! If he'd only complained about just one thing, it'd have been easy to remember. What the hells did Torf say again about that stupid short guard Glenn? Oh, wait, that's it, he's short... and he's sensitive about it!"

With a faint glimmer of hope in his eyes, Menderchuck waved to the advancing guard.

"I didn't know they let dwarves be guards!" taunted Menderchuck, shouting across the field.

Instantly, a wave of anger flashed across Glenn's face. Even from this distance, Menderchuck could see Glenn begin to loosen his grasp of the leashes. Fear is a powerful motivator, and it drove Menderchuck's brain into overdrive, trying to find a solution. And there, in some seldom used corner of his mind, he found it.

Long ago, his crafty grandmother had taught him that at times, when you're manipulating a person, you should tell them the exact opposite of what you want them to do. She called it reverse seismology. Probably, thought Menderchuck, because you could use it to move mountains.

"Release those hounds, short man," taunted Menderchuck.

Instantly, Glenn grabbed the leashes even tighter. No slave was going to tell him what to do.

"I declare myself to be free!" cried out Menderchuck for the world to hear. "If there are only children to hunt me, then I am a slave no longer! Best bring your dogs with you, boy, if you're going to have any chance to stop me."

Glenn gritted his teeth in anger.

"Now as a free horse rider, normally I'd challenge any servant of the Duke to a fight. Man to man, but I don't fight little children," goaded Menderchuck.

Irrational rage filled Glenn. His whole life he had been the butt of short jokes, and he was done with it. He was now a mighty guard. Slaves feared him. Those who didn't, he put in their place. Just last week he had smashed in an old slave woman's last two teeth as she laughed at him for falling off of his horse. It had felt so good, he thought, to see those two small yellow teeth fly out of her mouth and to hear her taunting laugh turn into sobbing tears.

"I accept your challenge!" defiantly shouted Glenn.

"Good, shorty," replied Menderchuck. "Bring your hounds. Then it can be a fair fight."

Like a Butarian sandworm, Menderchuck's words worked their way under Glenn's skin, traveling along his neurons until they were embedded deep inside of his insecure brain. The words rankled Glenn to his core.

"Down boys! Down!" commanded Glenn, roughly yanking back on the leather leashes with all his might.

With much struggle and cursing, Glenn dragged the baying hounds, against their will, back to the edge of the forest.

"I don't need you stupid bitches to put down an uppity slave," pridefully declared Glenn, firmly tying the hounds' leashes to the nearest tree.

Then he turned to face Menderchuck, who stood alone in the moonlit plains. Under the night sky with the hounds barking behind him, Glenn drew his sward from his scabbard and began to advance on Menderchuck.

CHAPTER 27: GLENN

The vicious sounds of the hounds' barking carried upon the wind, summoning guards from far and wide. The first to emerge from the forest was foreman Collins, riding upon his black stallion. For a moment, he brought his horse to a halt beside the pack of dogs. His brow furrowed with annoyance as his eyes beheld the knotted leashes which bound the baying hounds to a nearby tree.

"Sit," he firmly commanded through gritted teeth.

Instantly, the dogs sat down, becoming silent. Then the foreman heard noises coming from the moonlit plains. There he saw the silhouettes of two men who circled each other. Judging by the outline of sword and uniform, one was a guard.

Wasting no time, the foreman spurred his horse on towards the two silhouettes. As he did, other guards, who had been drawn by the sounds of the dogs, began to pour out of the forest and into the grassy moonlit plains. Quickly, they followed foreman Collins towards the two silhouettes.

Glenn's sword gleamed menacingly in the moonlight.

"Uhhh," sputtered the unarmed Menderchuck, slowly backing up. "Maybe you want to give me a sword too, sooo this is a fair fight."

"Oh, I'll give you this sword alright," coldly

threatened Glenn, breaking into a charge.

Like a coiled snake, Glenn lunged forward for the kill. Instantly, Menderchuck twisted his body, ducking into a backward somersault. The steel of Glenn's blade tore through the night air where Menderchuck had been only milliseconds before. As Menderchuck regained his feet, he was met with an unpleasant discovery. There, before his eyes, only a dozen feet away, sat foreman Collins upon his stallion with a host of guards in his wake.

"Awww, crap..." sighed Menderchuck, staring up at the foreman. "Howdy."

For a moment, Glenn the guard was a bit taken a back by Menderchuck's greeting. Curious, he followed Menderchuck's gaze, turning to discover foreman Collins looking on.

"Sir!" exclaimed a startled then resolute Glenn. "I've got this, sir."

If looks could kill, Glenn would have died at that very moment under the foreman's withering stare, but the foreman said not a word. Instead, he merely gestured to approaching guards to hold their ground.

While Glenn faced the foreman, Menderchuck frantically scanned the ground for anything that could aid him. Desperate, Menderchuck bent down in the ocean of grass that flowed around him, digging a handful of dirt out of the ground.

"Prepare to get cut down to size, slave!" loudly

taunted a grinning Glenn, pointing his blade towards the defenseless Menderchuck.

Glenn cut through the grass like a ship through the sea, recklessly charging Menderchuck once again. As the speeding guard approached, the barbarian dropped to the ground, kicking his leg out and tripping Glenn.

"Ahhhhh!" cried out Glenn as his body stumbled forward, colliding violently with the ground.

thud Came the sound of Glenn's head bouncing off of the dirt below while his sword flew from his hand, disappearing into the tall grass beyond.

"Glenn!" shouted out Adam the guard, who stood amongst the other guards that watched the fight with concern.

As one, a half dozen of the assembled guards broke ranks, rushing to Glenn's aid.

"Stop!" firmly ordered foreman Collins. "This is his fight. Stand down."

Like chastised dogs with their tails between their legs, the guards reluctantly returned to spectating. Face battered and bruised, Glenn pushed himself up, darting forward on all fours while Menderchuck pursued.

"Where is it?! Where is it?!" gasped Glenn, frantically combing through the grass for any sign of his sword.

crunch *crunch* *crunch* Came the ominous sounds of Menderchuck's approaching footsteps.

It was then that Glenn's terror filled eyes glimpsed the reflection of moonlight on steel. Like a rat fleeing a hungry street cat, Glenn scurried at full tilt toward the blade and not a moment too soon. In one swift movement, he gripped the sword's hilt in hand then deftly rolled onto his back, looking up. Towering above him was Menderchuck the barbarian.

"Eat dirt, dickweed!" yelled Menderchuck, throwing his handful of dirt down into Glenn's face.

"AGGGHHH!!" painfully screamed Glenn, dropping his sword, trying desperately to wipe the dirt from his eyes.

As Torfulson emerged from the dark forest into the moonlit plains, he heard the distant sound of his father's voice followed by the pain filled scream. To his horror, he looked toward the scream, witnessing the moonlit outlines of several dozen distant guards.

"Don't kill him!" cried out Torfulson's panicked voice.

As Torfulson broke into a distraught run towards the sound of his father's voice, Menderchuck and foreman Collins both turned towards the sound of Torfulson's cry.

"Utgh, utggh," painfully gasped Menderchuck, suddenly feeling the sharp bite of cold steel puncturing his lowered forearm.

A warm rivulet of crimson began to seep out of the barbarian's wounded arm. With a rough grunt, Menderchuck turned and looked down. There he was met with Glenn's dirty face which bore a great smug grin upon it. Though he still lay upon the ground, Glenn reached up, firmly pressing his sword into the barbarian's arm.

Like a volatile chemistry experiment, pride and pain combined, throwing Menderchuck into an animalistic fury. With reckless abandon, he lifted his right foot high. Then Menderchuck slammed his foot down upon the guard's throat, crushing it instantly with an audible crack that echoed out over the plains.

"Ewwww!" groaned out more than a few of the assemble guards, wincing at the brutal sound.

The sword fell limply to the ground as Glenn's hands grasped in vain at his crushed windpipe, trying desperately to breathe. Menderchuck, though, took no notice of the blade. Mercilessly, he violently kicked Glenn in the side of the face sending a scattering of teeth flying off into the tall grass that surrounded them. Then, with a ferocious finality, Menderchuck lifted his foot one final time. Like a wrecking ball colliding with a house, the heel of Menderchuck's foot violently stomped down upon Glenn's head, cracking it open like a watermelon in a shower of brains and blood.

It was then that a distraught and confused Torfulson reached the edge of the assembled guards.

"It's too late son, he's already dead," declared the foreman to the approaching Torfulson.

Torfulson held back tears as a tsunami of grief flooded over him. His entire life he had wanted a father, and now he was gone. If only he had been nicer to Menderchuck, when he'd had the chance.

"I get you were friends, kid," grunted the foreman in an annoyed tone. "But Glenn was a damn fool. Tying up those stupid dogs and trying to fight a slave one on one. You don't fight those animals on their own terms. He got what he deserved."

"Glenn?" quietly whispered Torfulson.

Emotions are not always logical. A wave of conflicting emotions collided in Torfulson at once. Though Glenn had been a monster at heart, he had also been one of the few people who had ever treated Torfulson as a friend. A guilty confused sadness crashed into fear. Fear of what the guards would do to Menderchuck in retaliation.

"Adam," commanded foreman Collins. "Go untie the hounds and search for any other escaped slaves. The rest of you, restrain this one."

"There are no other slaves!" interjected Menderchuck, grabbing his wounded arm.

Menderchuck's mind raced, grasping for straws in attempt buy Golgoth and Enok more time to escape.

"I fooled you all," exclaimed Menderchuck in false bravado. "You're a bunch of big fat, fooly, fools. I could fool you all day long. Knock knock... who's there? It's you, you dumb fool."

All of the guards, including Adam, paused as they watched the odd rantings of the bleeding slave.

"Alright, I'll bite," inquired the slightly curious foreman. "How did you fool us?"

"I infiltrated you. You didn't even know it, but I infiltrated all of you... wait, can I rephrase that?"

"Yes," coldly replied foreman Collins. "Please do."

Menderchuck raised his hand up high. It was covered in his own blood.

"I am Menderchuck the great! I will destroy you all!"

"You are odd, I'll give you that," replied the foreman, squinting doubtfully at the helpless barbarian. "Why would Menderchuck the great be masquerading as a slave?"

With a blank look upon his face, Menderchuck stared up at foreman Collins, "I'm not wearing a mask."

"Pretending! It means pretending you fool," cried out a tired and exasperated foreman.

"Oh, well I got a really good reason."

A silent pause fell over Menderchuck and the group of armed guards who now encircled him.

"Which isssss?" asked foreman Collins.

"Uhhh..." stammered Menderchuck. "I.. I have disguised myself as a slave to learn your weaknesses, and your schedules. And now that I have that information, I was going to summon my new warriors."

Menderchuck's grandmother had taught him that every good lie contains two elements. The second element is sharing something embarrassing. Most people will assume that you'd never share something embarrassing as a lie.

Menderchuck looked down, paused for a moment, and then meekly said, "But... I have chronic diarrhea. It stopped me here. I was pooing in this field, and I just couldn't stop. I think I accidentally parked myself over a rabbit hole. The rabbit, the poor unfortunate creature, came out of the hole and ran past me. I thought it was a brown demon... and it scared even more crap out of me. I tried to run, but my pants were around my ankles and I fell into... well, you know. I was cleaning myself off when I saw that man watching me."

Menderchuck pointed in the direction of Xerc's

corpse.

"What a crappy situation," dryly replied the foreman.

The guards howled with sycophantic laughter at Menderchuck's expense as a smug smile spread across the foreman's face. Menderchuck glanced toward the ground, trying not to smile himself. They had just bought his lie: hook, line, and sinker.

"Foreman Collins, sir," asked Adam. "You were at the battle with clan Chuck. Is it really him, Menderchuck the Terrible?"

"I don't know," replied the foreman. "It was a large battle, and I never saw Menderchuck myself, but Oleg will know. Guards, restrain this so called Menderchuck and chain him up in the barn. Adam, get your horse. I'll write you a message to take to Duke Belloch in Siztok. He'll be very interested to know that we have a prisoner who claims to be the great chief Menderchuck."

From all directions, the guards advanced, violently apprehending Menderchuck.

CHAPTER 28: THE MESSENGER

It was a well before noon by the time foreman Collins' messenger had reached Siztok's front gates. Adam paused for a moment upon his horse, gazing up in awe at Siztok's massive new outer walls.

"Urgent message for Duke Belloch, from foreman Collins!" declared Adam to the gate guards.

The massive wood and iron gates creaked open, and Adam was hurriedly waved through. He spurred his horse on through the surprisingly quiet and clean lower city towards the gates of the upper city. There too the gate was opened before him, and he was quickly waved through.

He spurred his horse on once again, speeding towards St. Ufstath's cathedral. Once there, he leapt from his horse, rushed up the cathedral's front stairs, and threw open its large front doors.

"Urgent message for Duke Belloch, from foreman Collins!" cried out Adam once again.

His voice echoed out in the quiet foyer. A stout middle aged man, who sat at a nearby desk, slowly looked up from his great stack of papers. There didn't seemed to be an urgent bone in the stout man's entire body.

"Do you have an appointment?" dryly asked the stout man.

"No, it's an urgent emergency message!" replied Adam.

"You need an appointment."

"How?! It's an emergency, you can't plan those!" protested Adam.

"Hmph," grunted the stout man. "You don't think I have work to do? The least you could do is show some consideration and plan your emergencies ahead of time. Now go take a seat over there, and we'll see if we can fit you in."

"Now you see here!" argued Adam. "I have ridden through the night and the better part of the morning all the way from the Westernson plantation with a message of top priority from foreman Collins for the eyes of Duke Belloch alone! I must deliver this immediately."

"Ohhh, in that case," replied the stout man with a nod. "Take a seat over there, and we'll see if we can fit you in."

For a moment, Adam opened his mouth to protest, but the disapproving look upon the stout man's face made him think better of it. Reluctantly, he quietly walked over to the couch, taking a seat. If time flies when you're having fun, then it slows to a crawl while you're waiting on the bureaucracy.

"Ummm, so," asked Adam after a few minutes that felt longer than most lifetimes. "Where is the Duke?"

"Ughhh," sighed the stout man, annoyed at having been distracted from his papers. "His main office is on the fifth floor. When called upon, you will go through the large door there, take a left, then head up the staircase."

THUD *THUD* *THUD* Echoed out Adam's footsteps on the cold marble floor as he leapt up and ran towards the large door.

"You're not going anywhere, son," smugly condescended the stout man, looking across the room as Adam grabbed the door handle. "The door is locked until..."

creeeaaak The smug look upon the stout man's face instantly turned to one of shock as Adam opened the door.

"No! Get back here..." screamed out the stout man.

Adam never heard the rest of the man's sentence for he was already bounding up the stairs towards the Duke's office. As he crested the stairs, Adam spotted two great doors across a wide hallway.

"That's gotta be it," exclaimed a winded Adam, rushing to the doors and throwing them open.

Adam froze in his tracks, overwhelmed by enormity and opulence of the room before him. Its vast walls were covered with exquisite swords, shields, banners, golden busts of the Duke, majestic paintings, big game trophies, and grand tapestries. Several sleepy guards stood at silent attention on either side of the doorway. A massive cherry wood table had been setup in the center of the room, and upon it was a giant map. Duke Belloch and Oleg stood around the table, studying the map.

It was then that Adam heard the sounds of footsteps and wheezing bursting into the wide hall behind him.

"Urgent message from foreman Collins," announced Adam, darting into the Duke's office and pulling an envelope out of his shirt pocket.

"No, no, no!" gasped the stout man, trailing Adam. "Someone forgot to lock the door! I'm so sorry your grace. He doesn't have an appointment!"

"It's fine, Bellamy," called out Duke Belloch, his voice echoing in the cavernous room.

The look on Bellamy's face said that he didn't think it was "fine" at all.

"Yes, of course your grace," replied Bellamy, retreating from the room, muttering to himself. "I mean, what's even the point of office hours if we just ignore them all willy nilly."

Adam stood there awkwardly while Oleg slowly crossed the floor towards him. As Oleg approached the messenger, he gave Adam a creepy wink and a smile, rudely snatching the envelope from Adam's hand.

"Oleg," began the Duke. "Stop messing with the

messenger. You can go, son."

Adam gratefully fled from the room. Oleg's creepy smile was bad, but his smell was way worse.

"Alright," continued the Duke.

Oleg stood there like a bump on a log.

"Open the letter, and read it to me," commanded the Duke.

riiiiiiiipppppp Oleg tore open the envelope as slowly as possible.

tap *tap* *tap* Duke Belloch tapped his impatient toes upon the hard marble floor.

At a pace that even a sloth would find interminably slow, Oleg reached into the envelope, pulling out its letter. Leisurely, he unfolded it, lifting it up before him. All eyes in the room were upon him, waiting in anticipation.

"Ummm..." stuttered Oleg. "I think I forgot my glasses."

"You don't wear glasses," snapped a growingly impatient Duke Belloch. "Now stop fooling around and read the letter."

"Oh, I forgot.... Well, errrr, uhhh."

"Yes, Oleg?"

"Ummm, it's illergitble."

"What?" asked the confused Duke. "Illegible?"

"Yeah, that's what I said..." weakly answered Oleg .

"Oh, I forgot. You dirty horse people can't read," replied the annoyed Duke. "Guard, take the letter and read it to me."

"Uh, I could have read it, if it wasn't written so bad," transparently lied Oleg, handing the letter to a nearby guard.

Karl the guard smirked to himself, enjoying Oleg's embarrassment. He was not a fan of Oleg. Most of the guards weren't in fact. Karl turned the letter right side up and began to read out loud.

"My dearest Duck."

Oleg and the guards tried in vain to hide their giggles.

"It doesn't say duck, you ignorant fools," exclaimed an exasperated Duke, marching across the room and tearing the letter from the guard's hand.

Duke Belloch looked down at the letter in his grasp. It did in fact say "My dearest Duck." He sighed and shook his head. Surely foreman Collins wouldn't have been stupid enough to insult him, but he surely was stupid enough to misspell "Duke."

196

"Why is everyone such a moron?" asked the Duke aloud. "No, don't answer that. I wouldn't want any of you to hurt your pea sized brains."

Oleg and the guards shuffled their feet in awkward silence. The Duke ran a hand through his hair, then straightened out the letter and began to read aloud.

"My dearest Duck Belloch,

I hope this letter finds you in good humerous. I alone have captured a mighty warrior who claims to be chief Menderchuck. We have chained and restained him, and await you're orders as to how we should proceed with him.

Your humblst servant,

~Forman Drake Collins"

For the first time in a great many days, a wide smile spread across Belloch's face.

"Finally, some potentially good news," exclaimed the Duke. "Karl, go flag down that messenger before he leaves. Tell him that I order foreman Collins to immediately execute the prisoner who claims to be chief Menderchuck. If he is the real Menderchuck, then we can't risk him escaping. Also inform him that Oleg and I will visit the Westernson plantation in three days so that Oleg may identify the body."

"Yes, your grace," responded the guard with a brief salute.

As Karl began to depart, Oleg took a step forward, blocking his path.

"Do you think that's the best plan?" Oleg asked the Duke.

"What?" replied the Duke. "Are you questioning me?"

"No, m'lord. It's... it's just that with a matter of this magma..."

"Magnitude?" interrupted Belloch.

"Exactly sir," answered Oleg. "With a matter of this magmatood, speed and discretion are of the highest order. We should only entrust the message to our most trusted servants, the palace guard."

"Fine, whatever," commanded Duke Belloch. "Karl, personally take my message immediately to the Westernson plantation."

The guard briskly saluted the Duke, departing the room.

"My horse is the fastest," declared Oleg. "I shall lend him to the guard, and help him prepare for the journey."

As Oleg sped after Karl, Duke Belloch wandered back towards his map table with a great smile upon his face.

"Finally, things are looking up," thought Duke Belloch to himself. "And it's good seeing Oleg pitching in."

CHAPTER 29: THE MESSAGE

Several flies buzzed lazily around the spacious horse stable. Oleg led his brown stallion by the bridle out of his stall and into the middle of the stable. Then Oleg carefully draped a blanket over the horse's back. With a small grunt, Oleg reached down and hoisted up a saddle. He then threw the saddle upon the stallion's back as the horse whinnied in protest.

"Yes, yes, I know," consoled Oleg. "You don't like the feeling of a saddle, but it's the only way the guard can ride you. Trust me, this will be worth it. I must see the life drain out of Menderchuck's eyes myself. I deserve that much."

As Oleg finished securing the saddle to his steed, the messenger guard entered the stables.

"Hop on," suggested Oleg, gesturing to his horse.

The guard put a foot into a stirrup and pulled himself up onto the horse. Then he grasped the reigns to ride off, but Oleg grabbed the horse's bridle and held it still.

"Not so fast," began Oleg. "So, what, exactly, is the message that you are going to deliver to foreman Collins?"

"Foreman Collins is to kill the prisoner Menderchuck immediately," replied the guard faithfully. "The Duke will come in three days time to identify the body."

Oleg's pride demanded that he correct the guard. It would actually be Oleg's job to identify Menderchuck's corpse, but he held back. Even Oleg was smart enough to occasionally realize that pride can be one's undoing.

"You got the message wrong," explained Oleg, staring creepily into the guard's eyes. "You are supposed to tell the foreman to keep Menderchuck alive. And that we will be there in three days time to execute him ourselves."

"That's not what the Duke said."

Oleg was prepared for this. He pulled a leather sack from his pocket. It clinked with the sounds of coins. Conspiratorially, he reached up and placed it into the guard's hands. The guard gave Oleg a quizzical look, then opened the coin sack.

"Wow sir!" gasped the guard who had never seen so many gold coins before.

"Shhh!" hushed Oleg.

"Yes, of course sir," whispered the guard. "The foreman is to keep Menderchuck alive, so that you may come and execute him yourself in three days time."

"Good," grinned Oleg. "Now get going."

The guard might not have liked Oleg, but he did like gold. And with that, he spurred on Oleg's horse, speeding off towards the Westernson plantation with a message not from the Duke, but from Oleg instead.

CHAPTER 30: VICK THE GUARD

The last light of dusk shone weakly on the Westernson plantation. Torfulson stood alone in the long cool shadow of the plantation's great barn.

"Menderchuck's trapped in there," thought Torfulson to himself, staring at the barn.

And it was true. Menderchuck had been locked in there since he had been captured the night before. Two men stood guard in front of the barn's doors. Torfulson instantly recognized one of them as Vick.

"Vick, let me take your place," entreated Torfulson, running up to the guards.

"Shove off," grumbled Vick.

"Do you really want to be working barn duty?"

"No," grumpily agreed Vick. "But we're under strict orders from the foreman."

"Well... then let me in the barn," implored Torfulson.

"Couldn't, even if I wanted to," shrugged Vick, pointing to the large metal lock which held the barn's doors shut. "The only way in is with the key, and the foreman has that. He doesn't let anyone in to see the barbarian unless he's here too."

"Ohhhh..." sighed a crestfallen Torfulson.

"Ugh, stop acting like a woman," groaned Vick, feeling a reluctant pity for Torfulson. "Your friends are trash. Glenn got what he deserved... but... you've always been fair to me. If it makes you feel any better, the foreman let some of the boys work the barbarian over, so long as they didn't kill him. Gotta say, that old barbarian sure can take a punch."

Torfulson winced at the thought.

"It's all so stupid," grumbled Vick. "This whole thing is. They should have just killed that barbarian king on first sight. Mark my words. You want a slave rebellion? Locking him in that barn is how you get them."

"You're such a cry baby, Vick," interrupted the second guard. "All you do is complain. It's not like we haven't put down a rebellion before. It's no big deal."

"That's easy for you to say," snapped Vick through gritted teeth. "Last time, you were all held up in the mansion, waiting for the Duke's army to arrive. I was stuck in the fields for hours, fighting for my life."

"Don't listen to him, kid," scoffed the guard, turning towards Torfulson. "Each time he tells this tale it gets bigger and bigger. He fought an old women and two kids."

"It was a dozen warriors!" argued Vick, flashing an obscene gesture towards the other guard.

"Don't listen to that pansy, Torfulson. Torfulson?..."

Vick turned to look at Torfulson, but he was already gone. Torfulson took in deep gasps of night air as he ran across the field towards the lights of the massively elegant plantation house.

"The key, the key, where would it be?" wondered Torfulson. "It's probably on the foreman, or in his bedroom... the bedroom!"

As a sudden realization hit his brain, Torfulson skidded to a halt. Foreman Collins' bedroom was on the second floor of the plantation house. It was rare for a guard of Torfulson's status to be allowed on the second floor. If he was caught there, he might get yelled at; but if he was caught there stealing the foreman's key, well, his fate would be sealed.

"I need an ally," whispered Torfulson to himself. "But who? No guard would help me. No slave would help a guard like me. Wait..."

Torfulson spun on his heels, turning his back to the great plantation house.

CHAPTER 31: GOLGOTH

As the first stars of night began to twinkle high above, Golgoth and Enok silently trudged along the plantation's lonely main road on their way to the distant slave quarters.

crunch *crunCH* *CRUNCH* Suddenly, the quiet of night was disrupted by the rapid sounds of hastily approaching footsteps.

"Wait! Wait up!" gasped a breathless voice from behind them.

As one, Golgoth and Enok reluctantly stopped, turning to face the approaching man. The man wore the purple of a plantation guard's uniform upon his body. A white bone handle knife hung from one side of his belt and a sword from the other. As the man ran, his left hand held the sword's hilt in place, preventing it from bouncing around.

"Huhhhhh, hhhhh," wheezed Torfulson, coming to a stop beside the two men.

The two men stood there obediently, waiting for the guard to catch his breath.

"Wuuuhooo," gasped Torfulson between deep hurried breathes. "Good thing you're so tall. Made you easy to find."

Golgoth the giant stood there in stony silence.

"You don't know me..." sputtered Torfulson.

"You're the guard Torfulson," interrupted Enok. "I saw you beating Menderchuck in the fields sometime back."

"Oh, umm, oh, uh, he wanted me to do that," flailed Torfulson. "It was a ruse. I didn't really hit him, but I was gonna. I mean..."

Golgoth and Enok exchanged a skeptical look. Things were not going as Torfulson had hoped.

"It's funny you mention him, haha," continued Torfulson with a nervous little laugh. "I need help with Menderchuck."

"How so, master?" asked Golgoth.

"The thing is, the thing is. Nobody else needs to know. I won't tell a soul. This will be between you and me. I already know all about you and Menderchuck."

A tinge of self preserving fear began to creep up both Golgoth's and Enok's spines.

"You want us to secretly help you?" asked Enok.

"Yes!" exclaimed Torfulson. "Oh, I was worried for a moment that you wouldn't, this is going so much better than... ack... ack...."

Torfulson strained to speak, but found no words. To his great surprise, Golgoth's massive left hand had wrapped around Torfulson's neck, lifting him from the ground.

"We don't collaborate," spat Golgoth, squeezing

Torfulson's throat.

Torfulson gasped for air, impotently trying to tear Golgoth's hand from his neck to no avail.

"No one can see you or hear you here," threatened Golgoth. "We're much too far from the plantation house, and the night is much too dark."

"I can see him," uttered Enok.

Golgoth glared down at his small friend.

"Sorry, I get it. I get it. I'm not helping," apologized Enok. "I think he's trying to talk though. Maybe you should loosen your grip some."

Golgoth thought for a moment, then turned back towards Torfulson.

"I'm going to loosen my grip just enough for you to talk," grunted the giant. "If you try to yell or scream, I will snap your neck like a twig. You wouldn't be the first guard to go missing from this plantation."

Torfulson nodded weakly while his face began to turn blue.

"Huhhhhhhh," wheezed Torfulson, gasping in air. "Father, Menderchuck's my father."

"What?" asked both Golgoth and Enok as one.

"Menderchuck," weakly croaked Torfulson, "is

my father. We planned on infiltrating a plantation in disguise to free his clan, our clan, from slavery, but we screwed up and came to the wrong plantation."

Golgoth the giant and his friend Enok exchanged confused glances.

"Prove it," muttered Golgoth.

Fueled by adrenaline and fear, Torfulson's mind raced for the proof that could save his life and his father's.

"I've completed the Kal Bartek!" cried out Torfulson. "Only a true member of the horse clans would know about that."

Though Golgoth's gaze remained as hard as cold steel, a glimpse of surprise crept into Enok's eyes.

"I've stolen my supper so that I could eat," anxiously declared Torfulson. "I've been to the horse merchant Evander. He's a right nut."

Both Golgoth and Enok nodded in agreement.

"I've learned to ride bareback," continued Torfulson. "I've been to the bad lands of Vetitik to face Verendu's favorite monster, the Chilopo."

"Alright, son of Menderchuck," began Golgoth, trying to trap Torfulson in a lie. "What's a Chilopo look like?"

"They look a bit like gigantic monster centipedes," replied Torfulson as horrific images of his encounter with them flashed before his eyes.

The hand around Torfulson's throat began to tighten once again.

"Wait!" gasped Torfulson. "Most initiates never see the monsters. The point of going to the bad lands is to face your fears and learn when it's wise to run away and live for another day."

"I'd say that moment has passed," threatened Golgoth.

"And... and..." stuttered Torfulson, his mind grasping at straws. "My sword!"

Torfulson awkwardly pointed to Menderchuck's sword which hung from his belt.

"It's Menderchuck's," pleaded Torfulson. "It's his great saber, Arbjak."

Hesitantly, Enok looked up to Golgoth, who gave a solemn nod of approval. As Torfulson's feet dangled above the ground, Enok reached up, pulling the blade from Torfulson's belt.

"It was certainly crafted for a horse rider of clan Chuck," explained Enok, expertly turning the sword over in his hands. "You can tell here, where the hilt meets the blade. But legend says that Menderchuck's blade is ten feet long, there's no way this is ten feet."

Torfulson rolled his eyes in frustration, "That's just hyperbole! No one has a ten foot tall sword. Your giant friend couldn't even wield a ten foot blade from horseback!"

"I have a name!" grumbled Golgoth, angrily shaking Torfulson about like a rag doll.

"Sorry, sir, I mean Golgoth. Golgoth, sir."

"You know," slowly uttered Enok, studying Torfulson's face. "He does look a tiny bit like Menderchuck. I think he's telling the truth."

Carefully, Golgoth lowered Torfulson back to his feet, freeing him from the giant's grasp.

"That's one strong grip you got there friend, I, I mean Golgoth," sighed Torfulson, rubbing his neck.

"Did you know that your father surprised attacked me from behind with a shovel?!" asked the incredulous Golgoth. "I ended up throwing him into a pile of horse manure."

"Well," replied Torfulson, "that would explain his smell."

"Yes, yes it did," laughed Golgoth. "Stunk up the whole shack for days. So, son of Menderchuck, why have you stopped us?"

"My father..." Torfulson's words faltered. "He's locked in the barn. It's only a matter of time until they kill him. I don't want him to die... I think I know where the barn's key is located, but I need help getting it.... please."

A pregnant silence filled the space between the three men as a cool night breeze wafted past.

"I don't know," mumbled Enok.

"He saved our lives," retorted Golgoth. "If it weren't for him, the hounds would have found us. It'd be us in that barn or worse."

"The hounds were only after us cause we were helping him out!" exploded an exasperated Enok.

"Still," firmly responded Golgoth. "Clan Dervin never forgets its debts."

"That's your clan, right?" asked Torfulson, praying that he was right.

"Yes," smiled Golgoth. "Now lead the way, son of Menderchuck. We have a debt of honor to repay."

CHAPTER 32: THE KEY

Somewhere in the distance an owl hooted while the stars twinkled far above in the night sky. Torfulson, Golgoth, and Enok crouched covertly in the lee of the massive plantation house. Quietly, Torfulson pointed up to one of the many elegant windows which lined the manor's second floor.

"I think that's the window to foreman Collins' bedroom," explained Torfulson in a conspiratorial whisper. "If I find the barn key in there, I'm going to throw it out the window, down to you."

"Why don't you just pocket it?" asked Enok.

"I don't know if they'll search me on the way out or not..." Torfulson's words hung in the night air. "And... well, if I don't get out, just make sure my father goes free."

Golgoth nodded while Enok put a reassuring hand on Torfulson's shoulder.

"Alright, let's do this," squeaked Torfulson in the bravest voice that he could muster.

While Golgoth and Enok hid in the bushes on the side of the great plantation house, Torfulson dashed around to the building's front. He leapt up the marble stairs of the massive porch in a single bound, then rushed across the porch, quickly pushing through its large double doors. His boots squeaked as he sped across the foyer's

213

decadent marble floor towards the grand staircase which led up to the second floor.

The sword on his waist rattled almost as much as his nerves as he gripped the large banister, leaping up the stairs two at a time. In no time at all, he crested the top of the stairs, emerging into the second floor's main hallway.

A plush red velvet carpet ran down the middle of the pristine white walled hall. A plethora of gold framed paintings hung from its walls. Expensive vases rested on marble columns that traversed the hall. On any normal day, these rich sights would have been the first thing to draw one's attention, but not today. Torfulson's focus was drawn to the two guards who protected the hallway's entry.

Like him, they wore purple uniforms with silver trim. Like him, they wore scabbards that held swords upon their belts. Though perhaps their swords were not quite as legendary.

"What you doing up here?" inquired one of the guards.

"Foreman Collins told me to come up here and tidy up his room," lied Torfulson.

"Hands up."

Torfulson raised his arms obediently. The guard stepped over and began to pat Torfulson down.

"My, you're getting friendly," teased Torfulson. "Slow night?"

"Oh, you don't know the half of it," sighed the other guard. "This is the most boring, assignment. Alright, you're clean. Go down this hallway, take a left at the first smaller hall. Six doors down on your left, that's the foreman's room."

The guard took his hands off of Torfulson, who then began to walk down the hall.

"Whoa, whoa, whoa," announced the guard. "Not so fast. You gotta leave those."

The guard pointed at the sword and knife upon Torfulson's waist.

"Seriously? The knife too?" asked Torfulson.

The guard nodded slowly. Reluctantly, Torfulson unbuckled his belt, handing both his father's knife and sword to the guard. Then he turned his back to the guards, power walked down the hall, and turned a corner into a small hallway. As soon as he was out of the guards' sight, he tore down the small hallway, eventually skidding to a halt before the foreman's room. There he paused for a moment, staring at the white door's brass doorknob.

"Please be unlocked, please be unlocked," silently prayed Torfulson, anxiously gripping the knob.

click A wave of relief washed over Torfulson as the doorknob turned in his hand. With a small creak, the bedroom door swung open. Quickly, Torfulson ducked into the bedroom, closing the door behind him.

"Wow," gasped Torfulson, gazing in awe at the room around him.

Never before had Torfulson seen such an elaborate bedroom. It was twice the size of the downstairs bedroom that he shared with his six roommates. The room's walls were covered in decorative gold leafed wallpaper. A great rosewood dresser, expertly carved with images of wood nymphs upon it, rested along the wall directly to his left. On his right, there sat an equally impressive mahogany desk which was covered in papers. And before him, dominating the room, was a king sized four post canopy bed that rested beside a small nightstand.

"Gosh," awed Torfulson. "You could fit a whole family in there, including the pets, with room to spare."

Torfulson shook his head, snapping himself back to reality.

"The key, where is it?"

He sped across the room, making a beeline for the nightstand. Roughly, he grabbed the handle, pulling it open.

"Nothing..," he grunted to himself, slamming the drawer shut.

Like a top, he spun around, then ran to the mahogany desk. One by one, he tore open desk drawer after desk drawer, rummaging through them, then slamming them shut.

"Ugh... papers, papers, papers..."

For the first time, fear of not finding the key began to outweigh the fear of being caught. Torfulson dashed to the dresser. As he pulled the top dresser drawer open, he came face to face with copious stacks of the foreman's folded underwear.

"Oh my, I didn't expect to be dealing with drawers in drawers," remarked Torfulson to himself. "Well.. ok... this is no time to be squeamish."

Torfulson shoved his hands into the drawers, pushing the clothes around. Desperately, his fingers searched around for the hard metal key, but they only found the softness of cloth. Drawer after drawer opened, and drawer after drawer closed, with no sign of the key.

"Where is it?!" exclaimed an exasperated Torfulson, slamming the last dresser drawer shut. "Where would I hide something so important?"

Instantly, Torfulson's eyes shot to the bed. Wasting no time, he dropped to the floor, desperately crawling part way under the bed in search of the key.

"Ugh, not here either!" grumbled Torfulson, groping around under the bed in search of the key. "Where can it..."

creeaaak The very words in Torfulson's mouth died a quick death as he heard the bedroom door open behind him. Awkwardly, he tried to hide his legs, which hung out from under the bed, but it was too late.

"Usually people make a bed from the other side," quipped a voice.

"Owwww!" painfully exclaimed a startled Torfulson, smacking the back of his head upon the bed's underside.

"Get out from under there," coldly ordered the voice.

With ice cold fear coursing through his veins, Torfulson scurried free of the bed. As he rose to his feet, nursing his sore head with one hand, he looked towards the sound of the voice. There in the doorway, blocking the room's only exit, stood foreman Collins. He wore an ivory handle sword upon his belt and a frown upon his face.

CHAPTER 33: BUSTED

Fearfully, Torfulson stood besides the bed, looking across the room at foreman Collins.

"I had a feeling I'd see you sooner or later," declared foreman Collins with a knowing grin. "Though I didn't expect it'd be under my bed. Move."

Timidly, Torfulson stepped aside, allowing the foreman to walk up to the nightstand.

"You were looking for this, weren't you?" asked the foreman, reaching under his shirt collar and pulling out a key which hung upon a chain around his neck.

Torfulson's blood ran cold while his internal fight or flight response argued in his mind.

"Scream and run!" shouted flight.

"Punch him in the balls, then scream and run!" shouted fight.

But Torfulson did neither. Silently, he stood there, eyes focused on the barn key.

"I know who you are," threatened foreman Collins, opening the nightstand drawer beside him.

The flight part of Torfulson's brain tried again, "Pee yourself, then scream and run!"

"You do?" squeaked Torfulson, before clearing his throat and recovering his composure. "You do?"

"Yeah, and I get it," responded the foreman, lifting key and chain from his neck and dropping them into the open nightstand drawer. "You're just a scared kid who wants revenge for your friend Gene."

"Glenn," weakly corrected Torfulson to no response.

"I used to have a friend too," the foreman's eyes grew distant as though looking back through the veil of time. "Archibald. We were thick as thieves. We made a living catching runaways. It was a good living. No one could tell a joke like Archie... but he was stupid, like your friend Gene."

"Glenn."

"There is no room in our line of work for ego, for laziness, for mercy," explained foreman Collins. "Archibald and I cornered a family of runaways who were hold up in a large brier patch. I don't know how they got in there, but neither of us wanted to crawl in after. The parents pleaded and pleaded that if we let their kids go, they'd surrender themselves to us. Stupid Archibald wanted to, but I knew better. I ordered Archie to stay guard there while I went to get some flint and tinder to burn them out. 'Archie,' I said, 'If one of them sticks their fool head out while I'm gone, just lop it off with your sword.'"

The foreman paused for a moment, his mind a million miles away.

"Don't take a genius to figure out what happened next," continued the foreman. "When I got back, I found Archie laying dead in a pool of his own blood. He'd been stabbed by his very own sword. No doubt he trusted those animals when I was away, and that was his reward for it. But the story doesn't end there."

"Oh?" asked Torfulson, whose eyes were fixated upon the barn key which rested in the open drawer beside the foreman.

"I hunted those animals down," cruelly smiled foreman Collins. "They weren't hard to track. Ambushed them as they slept. One by one, I killed them, making the others watch. I tore them apart, like a pack of hungry wolves finding a lone deer in the dead of winter. When I was done with them, well, no one would have recognized them. And then I dragged their mutilated corpses back to that damn briar patch, threw them in, and I burned it, burned it to the ground. So I get it. I get you wanting revenge for your friend, and were circumstances different, I'd probably help you. But this isn't our call. It's Duke Belloch's, so, no, you can't have the key."

With a great yawn that was earned from a long day's work, foreman Collins stretched his arms.

"If it's any consolation," finished the foreman. "The Duke is likely to kill that barbarian sooner or later. Be patient, it's just a matter of time. Now head off, I'm going to lay down."

Like a child trying to avoid bedtime, Torfulson's mind searched for delaying tactics.

"Umm, uh, sir," sputtered Torfulson. "Vick said we should be worried about a rebellion."

"Ughh..." sighed foreman Collins, trying to get rid of his unwelcome visitor. "Yes, as a guard you should always be wary of that."

Torfulson stood there silently, blinking dumbly.

"Look kid," continued the foreman, shoving the nightstand drawer shut. "I get it, you're worried, but there's nothing to worry about. The slaves wouldn't dare try me again. If there was a rebellion, just get to the plantation house here and you'll be fine. The thing is, our plantation, all the plantations really, are never more than a day's march away from the Duke's army. So you just have to hold out for a day at most. Usually it's much less."

"Wait," asked Torfulson as the gears in his head began to turn. "The Duke's army can make it to any plantation in a day?"

"Less than a day, if the roads are good," corrected foreman Collins. "It's a pretty clever scheme worked up by the Duke. The plantations are laid out like the numbers on a clock face. Each separated from each other, yet each equidistant from the clock's center. There, in the center where the hands meet, sits Belloch's great walled citadel of Siztok. If there's a rebellion at any one plantation, he can dispatch his army from there to put it down the same day, and no single plantation can defeat his army."

"What if all the plantations rose up in rebellion at once?" inquired Torfulson with a keen interest.

"Ha," chuckled foreman Collins. "You trying to give me a heart attack?"

"No, sir."

"Well," reluctantly admitted the foreman. "There's no way for the slaves to coordinate that. That's why the plantations are separated, but... for the sake of argument, if they magically somehow could, well, you and I would probably be dead. We'd just have to hope the army got sent here first."

"And the Duke?"

"He'd be fine. I'm guessing his army would just have a few rough days fighting from one plantation to the next. Worst case, he and his army would just hole up in Siztok, waiting to strike out again when the time was right. No barbarian army could get through those walls, and, judging by all the silos he's built in the city, he has years' worth of rations stored up... now, enough of this story time. I need to rest. You need to go. Shooo, get back to work," ordered foreman Collins, pointing towards the door.

"Yes, sir," dejectedly replied Torfulson.

Torfulson's shoulders slumped, and his feet dragged as he beat a keyless forced retreat from foreman Collin's bedroom. No sooner had he crossed the room's threshold, stepping out into the hallway beyond, when he heard the soft "click" of the door shutting behind him. To Torfulson, the sound echoed out with the power and finality of a funeral bell.

"Why does life always have to be so hard?" lamented Torfulson in a whispered sigh, desperately wracking his brain for options. "What do I do now? My soul is so very tired of failure. I can't go in there and fight him. He's got a sword. I got, nothing..."

As Torfulson's downcast eyes rose from the floor, he beheld the large painting which hung upon the wall opposite him. Like so much of the art that decorated the plantation house, it was pure propaganda. Contained in a garish golden frame, the finely painted canvas depicted a host of battle worn knights. Though their armor wore the scars of battle, their faces wore a look of pride as they admiringly gazed up at their heroic leader, Duke Belloch, who alone stood tall, dramatically lit by the campfire's flames.

"Wow," marveled Torfulson, stepping a half dozen feet across the hall toward the painting. "Whoever painted that really knew their constellations. Why, you can even see Arabeth right there in the night sky."

Suddenly, a commotion arose from beyond the hall. First the sounds of shouting, then the sounds of footsteps running his way. Hastily, Adam, wearing full guard uniform, turned the corner and burst into the small hallway, making a beeline for Torfulson.

"Where's the foreman?!" demanded a breathless Adam.

Torfulson pointed to the bedroom door behind him.

"Thanks," brusquely spoke Adam, before stepping to the door and knocking urgently. "Sir! Sir! The Duke's messenger has been fed and rested as you order. He's about to head back to Siztok, if you have any final messages for him."

"What? At this hour?!" came the foreman's exasperated response as the bedroom door flew open. "I thought he was leaving tomorrow."

"No sir, he insists he leaves yet tonight."

"Uggghhh," groaned foreman Collins, grabbing his belt; scabbard, sword, and all. "I got a host of papers I wanted him to take. Where is he?"

"Follow me, sir," responded Adam, darting down the hallway with the foreman in tow.

Silently, Torfulson watched Adam and the foreman rush down the hallway, then turn the corner, disappearing into the second floor's main hallway.

creeeeak Slowly, Torfulson turned his head toward the sound of creaking. There, before his ever widening eyes, the foreman's bedroom door stood ajar.

"It's open!" gasped Torfulson.

Through the open doorway, Torfulson's eyes spotted the bedside nightstand. Wasting no time, he dashed into the room straight towards the nightstand. In one rapid move, Torfulson tore the drawer open, ripping out the key and chain. Then he spun, tossing key and chain toward the room's window. Almost as though in slow motion, Torfulson watched the key arch over the bed, flying toward the window. *CLINK* Loudly reverberated the key, bouncing off of the closed window's glass and falling to the floor.

"Ahhh!" squealed a startled Torfulson, heart racing.

Instantly, he leapt across the bed, bouncing off of it and landing beside the window. Hastily, he grasped the window, trying to push it open.

"Open you stupid butthead of a window!" grunted Torfulson, struggling to force it open.

Finally, the stubborn window relented, flying open.

"Where is it? Where is it?" frantically repeated Torfulson, staring down at this feet. "There it is!"

Swiftly, Torfulson swept the key up in his hand, then shoved it out the window, releasing the key and dropping it below.

"OWWW!!!" came a distant painful shout from

below the window.

Quickly, Torfulson shoved his head out the window, looking down to the ground a story below. There he saw Golgoth nursing his head.

"Sorry, sorry, key?" whispered Torfulson as loudly as he dare.

Enok held up the key and chain in one hand and gave a thumbs up with the other. With a brief smile and a nod, Torfulson pulled himself back into the bedroom.

"The hard parts done," mumbled Torfulson to himself, beginning to rapidly walk out of the room. "Now to get out inconspicuously."

CRASH

"OwW!" erupted Torfulson in a self muffled yell as he accidentally crashed sidelong into the desk.

Hurriedly, awkwardly, he righted himself, power walking out of the room, down the small hallway, then turning into the main hall. At the end of the main hall, where it met the top of the grand staircase, there stood the two guards that Torfulson had passed earlier.

"Act like normal, act like normal," repeated Torfulson's mental mantra as he slowed to a normal walk and approached the two guards.

"Nice night," sputtered Torfulson, walking past the guards.

"What?"

"Yeah, you too," replied Torfulson before instantly feeling stupid.

"Hold on, stop," firmly commanded one of the guards.

Torfulson froze, right hand on the banister, right foot standing on a stair, and left foot hovering in midair.

"You're not getting away that easy," threatened the guard.

Torfulson slowly put down his left foot and turned to face the armed guards.

"At least, not without these," smiled the guard.

The guard held out Menderchuck's white bone handle knife and the blade Arbjak.

"Ohhh, thank you so much," groveled Torfulson, eagerly recovering both sword and knife. "I'd forget my head if it weren't attached."

"No problem, it happens all the time. Have a good night."

Sword and knife in hand, Torfulson turned, hurrying down the grand staircase to the mansion's foyer. As his feet landed on the foyer's marble floor, he rushed across the room towards the house's great front double doors. No sooner had his hand met the door handle, when he heard a voice from behind him.

"Torfulson!"

He let out an exasperated sigh, "What in the world, now?"

"Torfulson!" repeated the voice. "Come here!"

Torfulson turned to see Adam standing in a doorway across the foyer. Frantically, Adam gestured for Torfulson to follow him.

"I don't have time, Adam!"

"Come on, just come over here," suspiciously insisted Adam. "You're going to want to hear this."

CHAPTER 34: THE BARN

The dark veil of night hung over the immense sky which covered the Steppes of Rannsaka. Far below, the inhabitants of the Westernson plantation were preparing for their nightly trips to the land of slumber, well, most of them were. Two sleepy armed men stood guard duty beside the plantation's great barn. Little did they know that two pairs of eyes were watching them intently.

A massive ancient oak tree, whose leafy branches reached high into the night sky, stood but a short stone's throw opposite the barn. Beside the ancient oak, there rested an even older boulder. Like the oldest of friends, they silently enjoyed each other's company, having run out of things to talk about centuries ago. For the briefest of moments; the ancient oak, who was a bit curious about the two men that currently hid behind it, had thought about broaching the silence, before deciding it was best to leave his rocky resting friend in peace.

"Give me the key," politely ordered Golgoth, peeking around the tree towards the distant guards.

Silently, Enok shoved his hand into his pocket, retrieving key and chain. Carefully, he placed it into the giant's outstretched hand.

"Distract the guards, and I'll sneak in to rescue Menderchuck," commanded Golgoth.

Enok leapt out from his hiding place behind the ancient oak.

"Oh, and Enok."

Enok stopped for a moment, looking back at Golgoth.

"Try not to get killed," encouraged Golgoth.

Enok nodded, then turned away. From behind the tree, Golgoth watched as Enok ran across the dirt road towards the two armed barn guards. Though only faded snippets of Enok's conversation drifted back to Golgoth's hiding place, the guards beside Enok heard his words full well, and apparently they didn't like them. Instantly, Enok spun around, hightailing down the road into the dark of night with both guards in furious pursuit.

"Good job, Enok," whispered Golgoth to himself, leaping out from behind the tree.

The sound of feet running on gravel disturbed the quiet of the night as Golgoth darted across the road, skidding to a stop besides the barn's great doors. Quickly, he grabbed the great iron lock which held the barn doors shut.

"Come on, come on!" urgently whispered Golgoth, fumbling awkwardly with the lock.

click The key turned inside the lock, releasing its iron grip. In a flash, Golgoth cracked opened the barn doors, leapt inside, and then silently closed the doors behind him.

"Oh my," quietly gasped Golgoth, looking around the barn's massive interior.

Though the giant had seen the barn thousands of times in the course of his daily work, he had never seen it in this condition before. A small handful of lanterns hung lazily from the rafters high above, bathing the barn in a weak light that couldn't penetrate the barn's darkest corners. The barn's multitude of stalls, which were usually occupied by horses at this hour of the night, were eerily empty.

Well, most of the stalls were empty. On the far end of the barn, one of the stalls was occupied. There slumped Menderchuck, chained to the stall in a standing position. His head was downcast, his clothes were torn, and his body was bruised. As the remnants of hay crunched quietly underfoot, Golgoth quickly strode the length of the barn towards Menderchuck.

"Having a good time?" dryly asked Golgoth.

"Mppphhhhhpph," came Menderchuck's reply.

The captured barbarian slowly lifted his head, revealing a gag that was wrapped around his head and covered his mouth. Golgoth reached forward with single finger and carefully pulled the rag out from Menderchuck's mouth.

"Ewwww, yuck! It's wet," groaned Golgoth.

Menderchuck coughed weakly, "Is this a rebellion?"

232

"No, it's a rescue. Now, let me unchain..."

creaaak

Golgoth's blood ran cold upon hearing the creaking sound of the great barn doors opening behind him.

"Unchain mepphhpphphph!" exclaimed Menderchuck, struggling violently against his chains while Golgoth quickly forced the gag back upon his mouth.

Wide eyed, Golgoth hesitated for a moment, looking wildly about. Then he leapt into a nearby stall, dropping to the ground in hiding.

creaaaaaak

For a moment, all was quiet. Then fear gripped the giant as he heard the steady thud of footsteps walking in his direction. Laying prone upon the barn's dirt floor, Golgoth wriggled cautiously towards the stall's wall that was closest to Menderchuck. There he found a small gap in the stall's wood panels. Stealthily, the giant peeked through the gap at the intruder's lower half. The intruder wore the boots and pants of a horse rider of the clans.

"What? Who?" whispered Golgoth to himself.

Fear gave way to curiosity. Golgoth pushed himself off of the ground, stepping out of his hiding place to confront the intruder.

"Oh gods, you're a big one!" exclaimed a

startled Pavel, looking up at Golgoth.

"That's what your mom says," retorted the giant.

"That's not a very nice thing to say."

"You're right, I'm sorry," apologized Golgoth. "I've been spending too much time around this guy."

Golgoth pointed over towards Menderchuck.

"Menderchuck!" joyously erupted Pavel.

An elated Pavel ran over to Menderchuck, quickly pulling the gag from his chief's mouth.

"Gross, it's wet!" lamented Pavel.

Menderchuck smiled at the sight of his friend and bodyguard.

"I didn't know if I'd get here in time," announced Pavel, holding back emotion. "Now let's get you out of those chains."

creaaaak

Golgoth's eyes went wide for a second time as he heard the barn doors opening behind them once again.

"Noooo, unchaii...merppphph!"

Golgoth shoved the gag back into Menderchuck's mouth. In a flash, the giant grabbed Pavel by the scruff of the neck, dragging him into a nearby stall. There, the two men dropped to the ground in hiding. Once again, Golgoth wriggled to the small gap in the stall's wood panels. There he saw the trademark purple pants and black boots of a plantation guard. Slowly, deliberately, they walked towards Menderchuck.

"Guard," whispered Golgoth to the man (Pavel) that he had just met.

Cautiously, Pavel began to reach for the knife on his belt. Golgoth held up a finger for silence and shook his head.

"He might scream then," whispered the giant. "We need to knock him out."

Pavel nodded in silent agreement.

crunch *crunch* *crunch* Came the sounds of the ever nearing footsteps.

Golgoth and Pavel exchanged anxious glances.

crunch *crunch* *crunch* The sounds grew louder as they approached.

The giant held up three fingers for Pavel to see. He began to close his fingers one by one into a fist, in a silent countdown. Three, two, one, attack. Pavel leapt out of the stall first. With lightning speed, he punched the guard hard in the head. The guard yelled out in pain, collapsing to the ground.

"Owww! Pavel, why'd you do that?" whined Torfulson, laying on the ground, grabbing his head in pain.

"Sorry, sorry, didn't know it was you..."

"Wait, Pavel, what are you doing here?" asked a confused Torfulson.

Pavel reached a hand down, helping Torfulson to his feet.

"Rumor travels fast when the king of the barbarians is captured," replied Pavel, gesturing toward Menderchuck. "I came as soon as I heard."

"It's awesome to see you! How's Muffin?" asked Torfulson.

"Muffin is great. Yesterday she got into a carrot patch. You know how she loves her carrots," answered Pavel.

Torfulson smiled and nodded knowingly.

"MPpphpPHHHH!" furiously mumbled Menderchuck through his gag.

"Sorry Dad, let me get that gag," apologized Torfulson. "Ewwww, it's wet!"

"AHHH!!!" exclaimed an exasperated Menderchuck. "If you ladies are done with your story time, can you bother to unchain me?!"

Golgoth nodded in agreement and stepped

towards Menderchuck.

"Ummm... maybe we should wait a second," suggested Torfulson.

"Why?!" demanded Menderchuck. "Is it time for more 'pet talk'?! Maybe you have a squirrel that enjoys his nuts that we'd all love to hear about! Or, are we waiting for someone else to show up to this party?!"

"Maybe," cryptically answered Torfulson as the gears inside his mind began to whirl.

Golgoth, Menderchuck, and Pavel looked to Torfulson with keen curiosity.

"Golgoth," asked Torfulson. "Would you be willing to lead your people up in rebellion?"

All eyes fell on the giant.

"No," sternly replied Golgoth. "Duke Belloch's army is too powerful. There's too many of them. I won't lead my people to be slaughtered in vain, again."

"What if I told you that the slaves, our people, are spread across more than a dozen plantations. And if you combine them all, they dwarf the size of Belloch's army."

Judging by the look on Golgoth's face, that had piqued his interest. And so Torfulson explained to other men, what he had learned from foreman Collins earlier. As Torfulson reached the part about how the plantations were arranged like the numbers on a clock face, Pavel interrupted.

"That's true. That's how I got from plantation to plantation looking for our people, once I realized they're all arranged in a giant circle."

"Can we get out of here?!" urgently grumbled Menderchuck, pulling on his chains.

"Pavel," eagerly asked Torfulson, ignoring his father's words. "Have you been to all the plantations? Could you get to all of them in less than three days?"

"No, and maybe... I've probably been to most of them," explained Pavel. "Hypothetically, with Muffin's help, I might be able to get to them all. Why?"

"Adam just told me..."

"I hate Adam," rudely interrupted Menderchuck. "Now can you get me out of here!"

"Shhhh!" hushed Golgoth. "Go on, son of Menderchuck."

"Adam just told me," resumed Torfulson. "That he overheard from the head cook that she overheard a messenger from the Duke say that Duke Belloch and his army will be here in three day's time to watch Menderchuck be executed."

"All the more reason to get me out now!" gasped Menderchuck, his chains clinking as he wriggled against them.

"Normally," explained Torfulson. "If all of the plantations rebelled at once, the Duke could just hide in Siztok. Between its walls and his resources, he would be a thorn in our sides forever, a constant threat, even if we became free. To stop him once and for all, we need to catch him and his army away from his walled capital."

Golgoth and Pavel listened intently to Torfulson's words.

"But maybe, just maybe," continued Torfulson. "If we could catch his army away from the protection of the city, and we knew exactly where it was going to be, we could organize the rest of the plantations to rise up at once. Then they could meet, join forces, and march on the Duke's army before they realize what is up. We know where that army is going to be in three days time. Here to watch Menderchuck die."

"No! Nope! No!" argued Menderchuck. "Get me out, now! We'll figure something out when I'm free."

"Pavel," excitedly asked Torfulson, clapping his hands. "Do you think you can convince the rest of the plantations to rise up in three days time, then march on here?"

"I could try..." responded Pavel, deep in thought. "I have made some good friends at many of the plantations."

"Excellent!" erupted Torfulson. "Golgoth, what do you think? We're not going to have this chance again?"

All eyes turned toward the giant.

"Don't do it, giant," warned Menderchuck.

"If all the plantations rebel at once," sullenly replied Golgoth. "Then we will be butchered here, while the other plantations go free."

"That's why we stagger it," answered Torfulson. "Our job will be to keep the army distracted, which my father's execution will do, until Pavel can lead the united slave army here."

"Don't do it, Golgoth," protested Menderchuck.

"We'll need weapons, not now, but on the day," declared Golgoth, glancing around the barn.

The giant's eyes fell upon the barn's far wall. Upon hooks and pegs, in cabinets and on posts, a multitude of farming tools from scythes, to sickles, to shovels, to hoes rested, awaiting their daily use.

"Those will do," added Golgoth, pointing to the farm implements.

"Fine," agreed Torfulson. "I'll... I'll find a way to get the barn doors open on rebellion day. So, are you guys in?"

"Oh no, oh no, I don't want to die!" protested Menderchuck.

"You won't, we'll save you before that can happen," assured Torfulson.

"And if you don't?!"

Torfulson shrugged. This was the best plan that he could think of on such short notice.

"No, no, no," disputed Menderchuck. "You don't get to make this decision for me!"

"You're right," agreed Torfulson.

Menderchuck's chains clinked as he breathed a sigh of relief.

"Alright, unchain me then..."

"Show of hands," said Torfulson. "Who thinks that we should leave my father chained up as bait, and try my plan to destroy the Duke's army and free our people once and for all?"

Torfulson put his hand up.

"See, you're all alone," gloated Menderchuck. "Now unchain..."

Pavel cleared his throat, kicked at the dirt beneath his feet, then slowly raised his hand too.

"You traitor!" spat out Menderchuck.

All eyes now turned towards Golgoth the giant. Solemnly, he nodded, raising his hand too.

"You bastards!" erupted Menderchuck. "I'll

ki...mphhphppph!"

Golgoth forced the gag back onto Menderchuck's mouth.

"But what," asked Pavel, unsure of himself. "If I fail?"

"Don't," grimly replied Golgoth.

"It'll all be fine," assured Torfulson. "I... I mean a lot of people will die, but, in the end, we'll be free... the clans will be free... unless we die. I'm sure it'll work, and my father will be glad of it in the end. Don't you agree, Dad?"

"MppppHHhhhHH! MppppHHhhhHH!!!" came Menderchuck's furious muffled protests while he violently thrashed against his chains.

"Yes," declared Torfulson awkwardly. "I... I think that's a yes. We better go."

As Menderchuck screamed into his gag, thrashing impotently at the chains that bound him, he watched his son, his bodyguard, and a giant walk to the barn doors, then disappear into the night beyond.

CHAPTER 35:
THREE DAYS LATER

The unrelenting noonday sun beat down upon the great wide open Steppes of Rannsaka. A young defiant mouse proudly climbed out of his family's burrow and into the grassy plains beyond. No longer would he be subject to his parents' draconian rules. No longer would he be the victim of bedtimes, or having to eat vegetables that he didn't like, or having to share his toys with his younger sister. Now, he decided, it was time to make his own way in the world.

The mouse darted across the plains until he reached a nearby gravel road. There he paused, deeply breathing in the air of freedom. It felt good. Suddenly, the world began to shake. Fear gripped the small mouse. Hooves, then feet, much larger than the mouse, began to crash all around him.

"Ummmm, I think I left something at home," thought the mouse to himself as he quickly scurried back to the safety of his family's burrow.

STOMP *STOMP* *STOMP*

Came the sounds of thousands of marching feet.

CLANK *CLANK* *CLANK*

Came the sounds of thousands of canteens, weapons, and other accoutrements in motion.

Duke Belloch rode upon his mighty stallion. His sword clattered and swayed in its scabbard as it hung from his saddle. Oleg, upon his own brown stallion, rode beside the Duke. A column of hot and dusty soldiers followed in the Duke's wake. The Duke's army had been marching southwestward since dawn, and now they were approaching their final destination.

Duke Belloch pulled back on his horse's reins, bringing it to a halt. The sounds of the marching host went silent. The Duke's army halted in unison. Only Oleg, oblivious to this all, kept riding forward.

"Ahem," the Duke cleared his throat.

The sound instantly gripped Oleg's attention. Suddenly, Oleg and his horse found themselves ten feet ahead of the Duke, in the column's lead. Roughly, Oleg jerked back on the reins bringing his horse to an abrupt stop. Then he looked back at the Duke. The Duke said not a word, but instead raised a single eyebrow.

"Sorry boss, sorry boss," apologized Oleg, quickly spurring his horse.

Oleg's horse trotted back until it was even with the Duke's horse. Once again the Duke said nothing, giving Oleg a disapproving sidelong glance.

"Sorry boss," apologized Oleg again.

Oleg pulled back on his horse's reins. The horse retreated a couple steps backward until the

Duke's horse was in a slight lead. Satisfied with this outcome, Duke Belloch began to slowly turn his head, surveying the plantation's extensive fields around them. His brow furrowed as he lifted a hand to his eyes, shielding them from the noonday sun.

"Why is no one working in my fields?" asked a slightly perturbed Duke.

Oleg squirmed and gulped. He knew that this moment was coming sooner or later, when the Duke would begin to discover the truth.

"I don't know my lord," lied a groveling Oleg. "Perhaps they have planned a celebration in your honor."

For a moment, Duke Belloch gave Oleg a silent skeptical glance. Then he grabbed his reigns and spurred his horse forward.

STOMP *STOMP* *STOMP*

Came the sound of Duke Belloch's army once again in motion upon the road.

Twenty minutes later would find the Duke's army marching into the heart of the Westernson plantation grounds. There, fifty yards ahead of them, between the great plantation house and the plantation's main barn, stood a crowd of slaves. Obediently, the silent slaves waited beside the barn, surrounded by armed guards. Several armed guards also stood watch over the barn, including foreman Collins.

"What in the world is going on here?" asked the Duke aloud. "We're just here to see a corpse, that's no reason to stop work."

"I'll go check," suspiciously exclaimed Oleg.

Oleg dug his heels into his horse's flanks, spurring it on towards the great barn. Like an arrow shot from a mighty longbow, horse and rider darted past the Duke and through the center of the plantation grounds. Only at the last minute did Oleg pull back on the reigns, bringing his horse to a sliding halt only inches away from foreman Collins.

"Whoa! Watch out!" exclaimed the foreman, leaping out of the way.

Oleg leapt from his horse, glancing back towards the Duke's rapidly approaching army. Then he roughly grabbed the foreman by the arm, pulling him close.

"Is Menderchuck dead?" demanded Oleg.

"No," replied the foreman. "He's in the barn awaiting his execution, as the Duke commanded."

"Excellent!" erupted Oleg before catching himself. "I mean, what?!! You fool, you messed up. The message was for you to kill him, and we are here to identify the body!"

Fear crept into the foreman's face.

"That's not what the messenger told me!"

"Spare me your feeble excuses," threatened Oleg. "You messed up big time. The Duke will be furious."

"I, I... I could just sneak in the barn and kill him now," awkwardly suggested foreman Collins.

"NO!... no, no," refuted Oleg. "It's too late for that now. I can't condone lying to our lord."

"But... but..." pleaded the foreman.

"Don't worry," smiled Oleg, putting a reassuring hand upon the foreman's shoulder. "I'll try to smooth this over for you with the Duke, but we can't have this happen again."

"Oh thank you, thank you, thank you, it won't happen again," groveled foreman Collins.

Oleg turned his back to the foreman and began to walk, then run towards the ever approaching Duke.

"Sir," lied Oleg. "I have bad news to report. Foreman Collins is incompetent. He didn't kill Menderchuck as you ordered. Instead he's kept him prisoner and wanted to have him executed before you."

"What?!" erupted the Duke. "I'll have his head for disobeying orders."

"I agree my lord, but perhaps we should wait for that."

"Why?"

"A public execution could be good for moral," suggested Oleg.

Oleg gestured back towards the army.

"If the men," continued Oleg, "see your last great enemy killed before them, they will know that no one can stop you."

Oleg then gestured to the mass of slaves who stood quietly besides the barn.

"And," finished Oleg. "If the slaves see Menderchuck die, they will know that rebelling against you is hopeless. And, if I might be so bold as to say, you've been very stressed lately."

"That's true," agreed Duke Belloch.

"And, you know how you always enjoy a good execution," smiled Oleg.

The Duke frowned, "I can't have my plantation foremen disobeying direct orders."

"In a couple of days I'll have him arrested," suggested Oleg. "Maybe then we could have another public execution, but back at the capital."

"Oh, Oleg," smiled the Duke. "Just when I think you're a heartless barbarian, you go and prove that really care. You get me."

"What can I say? I'm a giving soul sir," replied Oleg with a small bow. "Now about that execution?"

CHAPTER 36: THE CONDEMNED

A curious raven fluttered her wings as she joined the great mass of circling carrion birds that flew high above. Like an unexpected family holiday, the raven recognized a host of familiar faces. Elder aunts and uncles glided effortlessly between distant cousins that the raven had not seen in years. Even her brother's crow girlfriend, who no one liked, had shown up. But more than that, in the midst of the great circling host which hung over the Westernson plantation like a black cloud, there were a great many faces that the raven had never seen before. Carrion birds that had traveled for miles and miles to get here, following Duke Belloch's army.

The raven's coal black eyes gazed hungrily down at the great congregation of people. For where there were people, there was food. Though, sometimes, people and food were one in the same.

A great group of dirty, worried, slaves stood forcefully assembled beside the plantation's great barn, encircled by a company of the plantation's heavily armed guards who were dressed in uniforms of purple. A massive oak tree, whose leafy branches reached high into the sky, stood but a short stone's throw opposite of the barn. Beside the ancient oak, there rested a large bolder. And dangling down from one of the oak tree's massive branches, there hung a rope which was tied into a noose at one end. Thousands of armed soldiers, wearing the distinct blue uniforms of Belloch's army, stood at attention in row after row of companies that flanked both sides of the clearing between the tree and the barn.

Three men (Duke Belloch, Oleg, and foreman Collins) rested in the shade beneath the ancient oak tree. Duke Belloch and Oleg sat upon their horses while foreman Collins stood on the ground beside them.

"Bring out the condemned!" dramatically cried out foreman Collins for all to hear.

A lone drummer began to play a death march as the expectant eyes of the assembled plantation guards turned towards the massive barn.

"Is something supposed to happen?" coolly asked the Duke.

Frantically, foreman Collins gestured wildly to Adam, who stood guard besides the barn's great doors.

"Oh, poop," gasped Adam, suddenly aware of the situation.

Frantically, Adam pulled a chain, which held a key upon it, off of his neck. Awkwardly, he fumbled with the key, placing it in the great lock that held the barn shut. *click* Adam breathed a great sigh of relief as the lock finally gave way. Instantly, he grabbed the barn doors, dragging them open one at a time.

There, revealed in the barn's massive doorway

was Menderchuck. Hair unkempt, wrists shackled to one another, body hunched, beaten, and bruised; a very humbled Menderchuck the Terrible sat upon an elderly mare. Two guards, one on each side of the steed, firmly grasped the mare's bridle.

Not far away, Golgoth and Enok worked their way towards the front of the mass of slaves who had been assembled to witness the execution. Silently, they watched as Menderchuck was led on horseback from the barn, across the dirt road, towards the ancient oak tree with the waiting noose.

"I put the noose up high," bragged foreman Collins with a smile. "That way we can have Menderchuck up on a horse, and then put the noose around his neck. When the horse runs off, Menderchuck will be pulled off and hang. Thought it might be poetic justice."

"Good thinking," replied the Duke, dismounting his own horse. "Maybe we won't have to arrest you after all."

"What?" silently mouthed the foreman, desperately looking to Oleg.

Oleg, though, ignored the foreman. As the two guards led Menderchuck's horse beneath the noose, Oleg eagerly brought his horse along side.

"I've got it," grunted Oleg, grabbing the noose and placing it firmly around Menderchuck's neck.

The two guards stepped back from the mare, allowing Oleg to take over.

"So, MenderCUCK," gloated Oleg. "How does it feel to lose everything? All those years I had to put up with your stupid rules. Putting up with you constantly thinking you were better than me. Denying me my right to take slaves. You cost me so much money. Well look at you now. You foolishly thought there'd be no consequences for crossing me. I arranged this all, just to watch you die. What do you think of that?"

"Did just you call me MenderCUCK?" densely asked Menderchuck. "That's not my name, it's Menderchuck. Did you not know my name all these years?"

"I know your name!" erupted Oleg. "You can't take this from me! I was making fun of you, you moron! Your stupidity will not get you out of this situation."

"Yeah," sighed Menderchuck. "That's what I'm afraid of."

Menderchuck's eyes looked up, beyond the horse he sat upon, beyond the road, beyond the assembled slaves and the Duke's army who stood in a circle around them watching intently. His eyes searched desperately for any sign of Pavel and his men, but they found none.

While Oleg taunted Menderchuck, Adam struggled, attempting to close the barn's great doors. Just as he was about to shut the second door, he felt a hand grab the door, resisting him.

"Wait," whispered Torfulson, holding the door open. "Let me go in the barn."

"What?" whispered Adam in reply.

"I want to watch from the hayloft," urgently whispered Torfulson, pulling the barn's iron lock off of the barn door.

"You can't take that!"

"I'm not having you lock me in there," replied Torfulson, opening the door enough for him to squeeze into it. "Just shut it and everyone will think it's locked."

Before Adam could protest, Torfulson, iron lock in hand, leapt into the barn, pulling the door closed behind him. Hastily, he hid the lock in a small pile of hay. Then he made a beeline for the ladder that led to the hayloft high above. Rung by rung, Torfulson flew up the ladder, emerging into the stuffy hayloft. Hastily, he snaked through the hay bales until he reached the hayloft's lofty doors which he threw open. There, from the hayloft's great heights, he beheld the plantation before him and the grassy plains of the Steppes beyond.

"Where are they? Where are they?" frantically mumbled Torfulson, scanning the horizon in vain for any sign of Pavel and his slave army.

CHAPTER 37: THE NOOSE

"Owww!" screamed out Menderchuck as he was pelted with a rock.

"I just invented a new game," grinned Oleg, tossing a rock up and down in his hand.

Cruelly, excitedly, Duke Belloch and foreman Collins began to grab stones from the ground around them. Together, with Oleg, they too began to mercilessly pelt Menderchuck. Bruises and welts instantly appeared upon the barbarian's helpless body as the hard stones ricocheted off of him. The horse, which Menderchuck sat upon, began to whinny and snort, startled by the rocks that whizzed above it. Fearfully, it began to inch away from the rock throwers, tightening the rope which hung around Menderchuck's neck.

"Whoa, whoa, OOOWW!!!, whoa," gasped Menderchuck, gripping the horse firmly with his legs as his neck began to be pulled back by the noose's rope.

Like a spooked pheasant, Torfulson darted across the hayloft towards the ladder, descending it at breakneck speed. In his haste, he missed the last two rungs, falling hard upon his backside onto the barn's dirt floor. Bottom covered in dirt and straw, Torfulson leapt up, rushing out of the barn's doors.

"Where's the lock?" whispered Adam as Torfulson rushed past him towards the assembled slaves.

Torfulson, though, had no time for Adam's question. As his father was pelted with stones only a literal stone's throw away, Torfulson made for Golgoth and Enok, who stood front and center of the mass of assembled slaves.

"You need to attack, now," urgently whispered Torfulson, approaching the giant and his friend.

"Did you see the army of our freed people?" eagerly asked Golgoth. "Has your friend Pavel succeeded?"

"Not exactly," stuttered Torfulson, who was met with skeptical glances. "You... you can't see everything from the hayloft. I, I.. I mean, yes you can see for miles in some directions, but the tree branches and the plantation house... and the forest in the distance blocks some of it. So... they could be out there. They're probably out there."

The eager look upon Golgoth's faced dissolved into a reluctant frown.

"That wasn't the plan," whispered Golgoth, gesturing to Duke Belloch's heavily armed army which stood opposite them. "If we attack alone, they'll butcher us. It's suicide. I can't lead my people to their deaths for nothing."

"It's not for nothing!" disputed Torfulson. "Pavel will be here."

"Maybe," reluctantly suggested Enok. "Pavel got

caught."

"No! no, no...," manically argued Torfulson. "No way."

As Torfulson and Golgoth argued, the mass of assembled people stood in a great square, intently watching Menderchuck and the horse. On three sides of the square, there stood the army of Duke Belloch; hot, tired, and dusty from a long morning's march. There they stood, weapons at their sides, watching at attention. On the square's fourth side, surrounded by armed plantation guards, there stood the plantation's slaves, the once mighty horse riders of the plains. And in the center of the square beneath the hanging tree, there stood Duke Belloch, foreman Collins, and Oleg.

"This is your beloved Menderchuck," loudly taunted the Duke, turning to face the mass of assembled slaves. "I like to think of myself as a kind master, but I must also be firm. Let this be a lesson to any of you who dare defy me."

With fear filled eyes, Torfulson watched the noose around Menderchuck's neck draw tighter and tighter.

"I don't think he has much more time," whisper squeaked Torfulson. "I've opened the barn, go get your weapons and rebel!"

With a heavy heart, Golgoth's eyes turned to the ground, averting from Torfulson's gaze.

Torfulson reached to his belt, past the sword

Arbjak, to his father's white bone handle knife. Stealthily, he pulled it from his belt, shoving it handle first into Golgoth's hand.

"Take it, and follow my lead," whispered Torfulson.

"Wh...acck... wh..acckk.." came the guttural noises from Menderchuck's throat as the horse stepped forward, and the constricting rope dug into his neck.

Whatever fear that Torfulson had had inside him that day was now overrun by a stampede of righteous anger. Anger at the Duke's crooked system that made free people slaves. Anger at the system that stole from the needy to give to the rich. Anger at the system that used people until they died. Anger at the system that rewarded the cruel and the greedy. And, most importantly, fury at the rich and powerful Duke and his cronies, who laughed as they were killing his father.

"Stop you bastards!" screamed out Torfulson.

All eyes turned towards Torfulson the guard. Pulling the legendary blade Arbjak from his belt, he rushed towards the clearing beneath the hanging tree.

"What is going on?" demanded the Duke.

Oleg shrugged in confusion.

"Torfulson, what are you doing?! Knock it off!" gruffly commanded foreman Collins.

Torfulson skidded to a halt several feet away from the three men, pausing awkwardly for a moment, not knowing what to say.

"No..." awkwardly sputtered Torfulson. "No... you knock it off. You all knock it off, right now!"

Like a lonely island, Torfulson stood alone, surrounded by a sea of on looking soldiers and slaves. Yet defiantly he stood, blade in hand.

As Golgoth and Enok watched, two familiar faces pushed forward though the throng of slaves, coming along side them. It was Inju the chieftess and Sven. Both were followed by the small remnants of their respective clans. Both of them flashed makeshift weapons that they hid in their hands, shivs made of stone and bone, then they looked towards Duke Belloch's men. Golgoth said not a word, merely shaking his head, instructing them to hold their ground.

"Who?" asked Duke Belloch, turning towards foreman Collins. "Who is this?"

"I am Torfulson, son of Menderchuck!" interrupted Torfulson. "Tell them dad!"

"Ackk.. acklll.." came more guttural noises from Menderchuck's throat, trying desperately to speak.

"See, he said yes...," announced Torfulson, raising the sword Arbjak triumphantly over his head. "And I don't stand alone! Alone I am nothing, together we are unstoppable! Men, to me!"

Silence was the only reply to Torfulson's dramatic call to arms.

"To me!... Men... me! To me!" lamely tried Torfulson again.

The soldiers, the guards, and the slaves watched on in still silence while Torfulson stood alone.

"Ha! Ha! Ha!" Oleg's boorish laugh tore through the silence as he began to slowly saunter towards Torfulson. "You're Lorelei's kid?"

Torfulson nodded.

"That's funny," continued Oleg. "Makes me feel like an old man, maybe we can talk this out."

"Free him first," commanded Torfulson, pointing his blade towards Menderchuck.

"Oh, that's not going to happen kid," explained Oleg as he neared. "Tell you what though, duel me. If you win, we let him go."

Torfulson nodded in solemn agreement.

"Great, shake on it," smiled Oleg, holding out a hand.

Torfulson paused for a moment, staring at Oleg's hand. Then he lowered his sword to his side. As Torfulson's hand grasped Oleg's, Oleg gripped tightly, suddenly pulling Torfulson towards him. In one swift move, Oleg brutally head butted Torfulson. Arbjak fell limply from Torfulson's hand while he collapsed unconsciously to the ground.

"You're as dumb as your old man," laughed Oleg, rudely kicking Arbjak to the side.

Dozens of feet away, Enok anxiously watched as Oleg stood over Torfulson's helpless body. Menacingly, Oleg pulled his sword from his scabbard.

"Golgoth, don't you think," urgently began Enok, turning toward Golgoth. "Golgoth?"

Where Golgoth had once stood beside him, there was now an empty space. Frantically, Enok scanned the crowd for his friend. Finally, he spotted Golgoth on the far end of the mass of slaves, approaching Adam, who stood guard beside the barn's front corner.

"Stop right there big guy," roughly commanded Adam. "Get back in line, or I'm going to have to teach you a lesson."

Adam pulled a truncheon out from his belt, wielding it threateningly towards the giant.

"OWWW!" cried Adam as Golgoth effortlessly slapped the truncheon away.

All eyes turned towards Adam and the giant. In one swift move, Golgoth lifted Adam from the ground. Then, as though his body were a bat, the giant swung Adam into the hard corner of the barn. To the horror of all the watching guards, Adam's head collided with the barn's edge, exploding like a gory piñata.

"Get him!" commanded the furious Duke, pointing towards the distant giant.

As one, the Duke's soldiers began to rapidly advance on Golgoth.

"Clan Oghul, on me!" cried out Inju, darting towards the barn with her clan in tow.

"The thing! Y'a know," grunted Sven. "Horse house! On me!"

Faithfully, clan Zetti rallied around Sven. Together, Inju's and Sven's clans formed a half circle, protecting the barn's entry way with their shivs. Valiantly, they fought, temporarily delaying the overwhelming army's advance.

Simultaneously, the multitude of assembled slaves, turned freed horse riders once again, burst into the barn under Inju's and Sven's protection, grabbing every sickle, scythe, shovel, and hoe that they could. Makeshift weapons in hands, the now armed slaves poured out of the barn like a roaring waterfall to make war against their vastly superior adversary.

As the forces collided all around him, Golgoth pushed through the enemy soldiers, making a beeline toward Menderchuck.

Eyes wide with fear, lungs screaming for air, neck burned by the rope that strangled it, Menderchuck's legs desperately clung to the horse. The horse was no war horse. She was but a humble farm horse. The shrieks and cries of the dying that now filled the plantation grounds filled her with terror. Startled, she burst forward, breaking into a gallop as Menderchuck fell from her back.

"Ughh!" grunted Golgoth, lurching forward and catching Menderchuck in midair.

With one arm, Golgoth lifted Menderchuck higher, allowing the noose a tiny bit of slack. With the giant's other hand, he reached into his belt, retrieving the white bone handle knife.

"You are nothing, but trouble," scoffed Golgoth with a small smile on his face. "Let's get you cut dow... akkhhhkkk."

Golgoth's words choked in his mouth, killed in their infancy by his desperate gasps for breath. With surprised eyes, he looked down to his chest. There he saw the metallic gleaming tip of a blood covered sword sticking out of him. Foreman Collins had run him through from behind. With pained shallow breathes, the giant turned from the wound and looked up at the rope that still hung around Menderchuck's neck.

"Let me go," croaked Menderchuck in a raspy voice.

Golgoth's eyes watered with pain as he felt the foreman pull his blade back out of his body. Yet like a mighty willow standing firm against a hurricane, Golgoth refused to drop Menderchuck to his death. Stubbornly, laboriously, the giant lifted the white bone handle knife toward the noose.

"Ugguhfff," grunted Golgoth, the sound bursting from his mouth in bubbles of blood.

Again, Golgoth felt the horrid sting of metal piercing through his body. Again, the foreman's blade erupted through the front of Golgoth's torso releasing a river of blood. And again, Golgoth felt the horrid agony of the blade being pulled back out of his body.

In one pained motion, Golgoth dragged the knife's blade across the noose's rope, cutting Menderchuck free. As Golgoth began to lower Menderchuck, the foreman's blade pierced him from behind for a third time. For a moment, Golgoth moved his lips to speak, but no words came out. Drenched in his own blood, the giant staggered to his knees, carefully placing Menderchuck down. Then, with one final gasp, Golgoth the giant collapsed to the ground to breathe no more.

"Golgoth!" screamed out Enok with tears in his eyes.

Heart full of anguish, Enok pushed his way through the fighting towards his friend's distant corpse.

"You," grunted foreman Collins, turning toward Enok's scream. "You will all pay for this!"

Threateningly, foreman Collins lifted his sword, advancing upon the unarmed Enok.

"I'm going to chop you into... AHHHHH!" screamed foreman Collins, suddenly stumbling forward.

Though Menderchuck lay on the ground, wrists bound, he had managed to kick his leg out, tripping the foreman. As foreman Collins stumbled forward then regained his balance, Enok darted past him. In one swift move, Enok skidded to a halt upon his knees beside the white bone handle knife. Quickly, he grasped it in his hand, leapt to his feet, then turned to face the foreman once more.

"Nice tooth pick slave," taunted the foreman, pointing his sword towards Enok. "What are you going to do, clean my teeth for me, Awkkkkkghhh...."

Foreman Collins eyes widened, and his mouth went a gape. To his surprise, the white bone handle knife was now embedded in his arm. Enok had thrown it with lighting quick speed. The foreman dropped his sword, pulling the bloody knife from his arm.

"Coward!" angrily spat the foreman, dropping the knife upon the ground.

Then foreman Collins spun rapidly around, fleeing for dear life towards the great plantation house with Enok hot on his tail.

With an exhausted sigh, Menderchuck sat up, lifting his shackled hands and pulling the remnants of the noose off of his rope burned neck.

"I'm sorry..." quietly whispered Menderchuck,

looking over at the once mighty giant's lifeless body.

As the battle closed in around him, Menderchuck ducked and rolled to avoid being trampled. And then he saw it, only ten feet away, his beloved Arbjak. Menderchuck's clinking chains could not be heard over the din of battle as he crawled rapidly between combatants' legs toward his legendary blade. No sooner had he gripped the hilt of his trusty sword, then he brought it up to his face.

"It's good to see you, old friend," he said to the blade with a kiss.

Menderchuck, sword in hand, scurried to the boulder beside the ancient oak tree. There he placed his chains upon the rock, smashing them apart with Arbjak's pommel. Then he stood tall, turning to face the battle.

Before him, a great multitude of slaves, soldiers, and guards were locked in a desperate struggle between life and death. Though his fellow horse riders were poorly armed and out numbered, they were putting up a valiant, but losing struggle. Menderchuck then lifted his sword high and waded into battle in search of Oleg.

CHAPTER 38: ENOK

The great plantation house's large double doors flew open as foreman Collins hastily burst into the house's majestic foyer. Eyes wide with fear, the foreman frantically spun around, slamming the doors shut and locking them behind him. Blood dripped down his wounded arm, splattering into a small puddle upon the hard marble floor below.

BAM *BAM* *BAM* Came the disturbing sound of someone violently crashing into the house's double doors immediately before him. Like a scared mouse, the foreman's footsteps rapidly echoed off of the marble floor while he scurried across the room, fleeing towards the grand staircase. Two at a time, foreman Collins bound up the stairs, never daring to look back towards the pounding sounds which resonated menacingly off of the house's front doors. He didn't need to. He knew who pursued him.

"Open, open, damn you!" grunted Enok, recklessly slamming the weight of his entire body into the double doors for a sixth time.

With the savage crack of splintering wood, the doors gave way, bursting open. Enok erupted into the entry hall, eyes darting furiously about in pursuit of his quarry. Then he saw it, for just a moment, at the top of the stairs. There was the back of the foreman, who quickly disappeared into the second floor hall above.

Enok darted across the marble floor to the grand

staircase, rushing up its stairs. As he crested the final stair, Enok stopped again. Before him was a grand hall. Its walls were covered with row after row of doors which were occasionally interrupted by off shoots of smaller hallways.

"Where are you?!" cried out Enok. "I will find you, if I have to search every room!"

The sound of his own voice echoing down the empty hall was his only response. Anxiously, Enok looked to the left for any sign of the foreman, but saw nothing. He looked to the right and still saw nothing. Then he glanced to his feet. There he spotted a trail of blood leading up the main hall and turning down a smaller hallway.

Foreman Collins dashed into his bedroom, shutting the door as quietly as possible behind him. Then he rushed around to the side of his large rosewood dresser. Placing the shoulder of his uninjured arm into the side of the dresser, he began to push with all of his might.

"You can run! But I will hunt you to hell!" came the terrifying shout of Enok's ever nearing voice.

The icy stab of fear penetrated the foreman's heart. The cold sweat of fragile mortality dripped off of his brow while the dresser began to slide forward under his weight. It was just in the nick of time. No sooner had the massive dresser blocked the bedroom's only door, when the foreman heard the ominous rattle of the doorknob turning.

thud *thud* *thud* Banged out the door, colliding with the immovably massive dresser which barred its path. *THUD* *THUD* *THUD* Crashed out the door as Enok repeated tried in vain to force it open. Yet the heavy rosewood dresser refused to yield even a single inch.

"Ha, ha, idiot," taunted foreman Collins, breaking into a relieved laughter.

Then the foreman cautiously slid to ground, sitting with his back to the dresser. Gingerly, he lifted his free hand to his bloody injured arm, nursing the wound.

bam "Owww!" painfully cried out Enok, trying unsuccessfully to kick the door in.

As Enok heard a hearty laugh from beyond the door, he furrowed his brow and began to manically pace up and down the small hallway.

"There's gotta be a way in there. There's gotta be a way in there, but how?" muttered Enok to himself over and over again.

Clutching at straws, Enok threw open the door of an adjacent empty bedroom. Stepping inside, his eyes scoured the room for aid. He looked over to the canopy bed, nothing. He looked over to the dresser, nothing. He looked over to the nightstand, nothing. Then his eyes fell upon the room's fireplace.

"That's it!" erupted Enok, rushing towards the fireplace.

Sitting upon the fireplace mantle was a lamp, a flint, and a rod of steel. Hastily, Enok grabbed all three, then rushed back into the small hallway, placing the three items at the base of the foreman's barred door.

Up and down the hallway, left and right, unlocked bedroom doors flew open as Enok burst into them, retrieving their lamps. In no time at all, he had a amassed a collection of more than a dozen lamps which now lay outside of the foreman's door.

crash *smash* *crash*

From inside his room, the foreman smugly smiled as he heard impotent crashing upon his door.

"Nice try loser," shouted the taunting foreman. "You're never getting in here."

"I don't intend to," grinned Enok to himself, smashing the last lamp upon the foreman's door.

Copious amounts of lamp oil poured down the foreman's door, flowing past the shard's of lamp glass which covered the floor, seeping into the carpet that ran the length of the small hallway. Enok scurried to the edge of the carpet's growing oil stain, crouching down with flint and steel in hand.

clink *clink* *clink* Came the sound of steel striking flint.

A small shower of sparks erupted from the flint

269

in Enok's hand, raining down upon the oil puddle below.

WHOOOSH Exploded the sound of a great ball of fire which burst into life before him.

"Oh my!" gasped Enok, bowled back by the intense waves of heat which emanated from the conflagration.

Like an elemental horse race, a fierce wall of flames raced down the hallway along the oil soaked carpet towards the foreman's door. Beating a hasty retreat to the small hallway's entrance, Enok intently watched the growing fire before him. Higher and higher, the flames climbed along the hallway's walls. Faster and faster, they shot down the hall, greedily consuming all before it. While priceless paintings honoring Duke Belloch burned on the plantation house's walls, the hungry flames began to climb up the foreman's bedroom door. It was then that Enok turned his back to the fire and ran.

As the sounds of smashing upon his door died down, foreman Collins, who still sat upon the floor, smiled contentedly to himself.

"Coward, of course he'd give up," triumphantly grinned the foreman.

sniff *sniff*

"What's that?" he wondered aloud.

sniff *sniff* The foreman's eyes went wide as

his nose detected the smell of smoke.

"No.. no..."

With his good arm, foreman Collins braced himself against the dresser, pushing himself up to his feet. Whiffs of visible smoke began sneak under the door, penetrating the room. Franticly, foreman Collins rushed to the opposite side of his rosewood dresser.

bang "Owww!"

In his haste, the foreman accidentally slammed into his nearby desk. The desk stood besides the moved dresser, preventing the foreman from placing his shoulder upon it. Desperately, foreman Collins reached out with his good hand at an oblique angle, pulling with all his might upon the dresser. Yet the dresser stubbornly refused to move.

"Awwkkghg, Agghhkkk," roughly coughed the foreman as the smoke that rapidly filled the room began to fill his lungs.

Stumbling forward, foreman Collins rushed through the smoky haze to the window. Using his good arm, he fumbled awkwardly with it for a moment before throwing it open. Billows of smoke escaped the bedroom, pouring out of the now open window. Hurriedly, the foreman shoved his head out of the window, desperately gasping in the fresh air. As his deep breaths turned into a slow panting, oxygen began to return to his lungs.

"I need to get down th..." foreman Collin's words stuck in his throat.

Shocked, foreman Collins looked down from his second story window to the ground below. There, standing upon the ground below, looking back up at him, was Enok.

"Can we discuss this?!" pleaded foreman Collins, calling down to Enok. "I can give you your freedom. Just let me climb down!"

Enok said not a word. Instead he silently glared up at the foreman, patiently waiting. Hopelessly, the foreman glanced back into his smoke filled room.

"No! No... no..." gasped the foreman, seeing that the room's only door was now engulfed in flames.

Like a fiery rising tide, flames began to roll across the floor, bursting into a ball of fire as they reached the room's canopy bed. The deafening roar of flames assaulted the foreman's ears, and the heat of its fire blistered his skin. Spurred on by the animalistic drive of self preservation, foreman Collins awkwardly began to climb out of the second floor window.

"AhhhHHHH!" gasped the foreman, legs dangling precariously out of the window.

His heart skipped a beat until his toes found footing upon the small decorative ledge that ran the length of the second story. Finding his balance, the foreman began to slowly shimmy upright along the house's outer ledge. No sooner had the foreman cleared the window, when flames began to erupt from it. His face grimaced while his wounded arm brushed against the plantation house's outer wall, creating a grim trail of blood.

"OWW!" screamed out foreman Collins, suddenly feeling the harsh sting of a rock smashing into the side of his body.

The knuckles of his good arm's hand went white, clinging defiantly to the edge of the window's molding while he precariously balanced himself upon the tiny ledge.

"Like my new game?" taunted Enok from below, hurling another stone up at the foreman.

The sound of stone cracking rib was covered by the sound of the foreman's pained cry. Yet he stubbornly held to the window's molding for dear life. Pelting stone after pelting stone was followed by cry after cry.

"Stop, you bastard!" furiously shouted foreman Collins. "I should have killed all of you animals when I had the chance!"

Enok looked down at his feet and picked up another stone. Only three nights before, he and Golgoth had stood under this very window. With a steely gaze, Enok looked up at foreman Collins once more.

"This is for my friend!" defiantly shouted Enok.

The stone flew from Enok's hand, speeding up through the air, and smashing into foreman Collin's good hand. *CRAACK* The bones in the middle of his hand shattered on impact.

"AGGHHHH!" screamed out the foreman, losing grip of the window's molding.

For a fraction of a second, the foreman maintained his delicate balance upon the tiny ledge, and then he fell. His body plummeted to the ground below, landing on his head with a bone shattering crunch. While roaring flames flickered above, Enok stepped over foreman Collins' lifeless body.

CHAPTER 39: RAGING INFERNO

The desperate sounds of guards, soldiers, and slaves locked in mortal combat rang throughout the plantation grounds. Great roaring waves of fire rushed up the sides of the opulent plantation house while flames of rage filled Menderchuck's soul. There, thirty feet away, backlit by the glow of the raging inferno, Menderchuck locked eyes with the traitor who had destroyed the better part of his family and his clan.

"Oleg," grunted Menderchuck, wincing as he tried to hold back the crushing anguish which filled his tormented soul.

Like two great and furious grizzly bears, the two barbarians charged each other. Violently, they collided with the mighty clang of steel. A shower of sparks rained down from both men's blades as they furiously crashed into each other, again and again.

Some sword fights are quiet cerebral moments of opponents looking for an opening, then taking it. This was not such a fight. This was a blur of unbridled animalistic fury. Neither man fought merely to win or to maim the other. Both men fought with the sole intent to kill.

"Uggh..." gasped Oleg, trying to catch his breath as he desperately parried another of Menderchuck's attacks.

Over the course of his lifetime, Oleg had seen Menderchuck fight many times on many raids and in many battles, but he had never been on the receiving side of such vicious fury. Again and again the two forces collided, like a hammer hitting an anvil. With each brutal attack, Menderchuck seemed to grow stronger while Oleg seemed to grow weaker.

As Oleg's energy flagged, so too did his guard. The traitor's blade drooped for only a fraction of a second, but it was enough time for Menderchuck to find his opening. With the speed of a viper and a bone shattering crack, Menderchuck smashed his hilt into the side of Oleg's head.

"AGGGHHH!" painfully cried out Oleg, recoiling backwards from the brutal blow.

Oleg's saber dropped from his hand, falling to the ground, while he grasped his now bleeding head with both hands. Menderchuck paused his attack for a moment, looking Oleg dead in the eyes.

"Die, traitor," commanded Menderchuck.

Blood running down the side of his head and over his fingers, Oleg grunted with a toothy defiant grin.

"Kill me, if you dare," taunted Oleg. "But if you kill me, then I really have taken everything from you. I win. If you kill me, then you kill the last of your clan. The last of your blood. The last of your people. You will be alone in the world."

"No," refuted Menderchuck. "I have a son."

Menderchuck lifted his mighty blade Arbjak above the defenseless Oleg. As he did, Oleg held up his arm to defend himself from the blow. *CRAAACK* Menderchuck's blade sliced right through Oleg's arm, loping off the hand and part of the forearm. As the sound of breaking bone filled the air, massive squirts of blood rained out from Oleg's stumpy arm. Yet Arbjak's blade continued its terrifying swing, plunging deep into Oleg's body where his neck met his torso.

"Ugghh, come on," grunted Menderchuck, trying to pull his blade from Oleg's body, but it was stuck fast.

Annoyed, Menderchuck jerked the blade's handle repeatedly, but it wouldn't budge. With each pull, Oleg's upper torso just flailed back and forth.

Oleg opened his mouth to gasp for air, but received none. The blade had severed his windpipe. In confused terror, Oleg looked up at Menderchuck, who was growing quite frustrated at not being able to remove his blade from Oleg's body.

"Don't move," absentmindedly commanded Menderchuck almost as though working on a project with a friend.

Then Menderchuck placed one foot on Oleg's chest and pushed with his leg. At the same time, he pulled with all his might on the blade's hilt.

"Come on! Get out of him!" grunted

Menderchuck, veins popping as he strained to free his blade.

pop Suddenly the blade flew free and Menderchuck stumbled backwards, falling to the ground. It was then that he looked over to Oleg, who was covered in blood. For a moment, Oleg teetered from side to side, then he collapsed to the ground. Laying upon his back, Oleg slowly blinked twice, watching the mass of carrion birds which circled high above. Then, like the copious amounts of blood that gushed from his severed arm and neck, the final drops of life drained from Oleg's body.

"Uggggh," wearily groaned Menderchuck, pushing himself up into a sitting position while the sounds of battle clambered just a stone's throw away.

Pain, what Menderchuck felt now was pain. The vindicated relief of long sought revenge mixed with righteous anger and the heavy anguish of loss, creating a terrible emotional cocktail. And so he drank, unwillingly, from this cocktail of sadness. Great sadness at the loss of his clan, at the loss of most of his family, at the betrayal of a man that he had once called friend. He felt an overwhelming emotional pain, and then he felt an overwhelming physical pain.

It had happened so quickly that Menderchuck was caught unawares. For as he sat there, wresting with emotion for the briefest of seconds, Duke Belloch had snuck up behind him. The Duke lifted his sword high above Menderchuck. In one swift downward blow, the full force of the Duke's sword sliced Menderchuck's left arm clean off just below the shoulder.

"AAGHHGH!" painfully gasped Menderchuck, reflexively reaching his right hand over to grasp his left arm.

To Menderchuck's horror and surprise, his left arm was no longer there. Bleeding and writhing in pain, Menderchuck fell back upon the ground. It was then that he looked up and saw Duke Belloch standing menacingly over him.

"You stupid backwards son of a bitch," spat out the enraged Duke. "I am going to make something out of this hellhole of a country, despite you people!"

The Duke raised his blade to deliver the killing blow while Menderchuck helplessly watched.

CRAAASH

Suddenly, Duke Belloch was bowled over by a charging Pavel, who rode upon Muffin the donkey. The Duke's blade flew from his hand, landing in the dirt several feet away. Pavel, who was unarmed, leapt from Muffin's back, charging Duke Belloch. The two men collided, awkwardly punching and gouging each as they rolled together upon the ground.

Quickly, Duke Belloch gained the upper hand, twisting his body's weight, pinning down Pavel. It was then that Pavel unleashed his secret weapon. Viciously, Pavel reached up and grabbed the Duke by his hair, yanking it as hard as he could.

"OWWWW!" howled out the Duke in pain. "You can't do that!"

Pavel smiled to himself. Finally, having grown up with many sisters was paying off. But Pavel's smile didn't last long. The Duke bent his own leg back towards his torso, reaching into his boot and retrieving a cruel looking dagger with a curved blade.

"AHHH!!" yelped Pavel, feeling the sting of the knife being plunged deep into his thigh.

While Pavel recoiled in pain, Duke Belloch leapt to his feet, scrambling over to his sword which now lay a half dozen feet away. No sooner had Duke Belloch gripped his sword in hand and turned, when he witnessed Pavel, knife still stuck in his bleeding leg, slowly climb to his feet.

Face filled with a determined fury, Pavel's fingers wrapped around the knife's handle. With a grimace, a grunt, and a deep pained breath, Pavel pulled the blade from his leg, unleashing rivulets of blood that poured from the wound and stained his clothes.

Like a flash of lighting, Pavel hurled the knife at Duke Belloch. *tink* With the expert precision of years of practice, Duke Belloch effortlessly parried the flying blade with his sword. The knife clattered harmlessly to the ground only a few feet away.

"Look dirt eater," condescended the Duke. "I'm a master swordsman with a sword, and you're a dirt eater, with nothing. Surrender, and I'll let you live."

Defiantly, Pavel spat at the Duke. It flew in a wide arch through the air, then hit the Duke in the face in a big wet mess.

"EWWW!!! Why are you barbarians so inbred stupid?!?!" demanded the Duke, raising his blade to charge Pavel.

"PAVEL!" screamed out a voice from behind the Duke.

Startled, the Duke spun around to see Torfulson standing there in his guard's uniform. It was torn and smattered in blood. In Torfulson's hand, he held Arbjak, the sword of his father.

"Pavel!" screamed out Torfulson again. "Take care of my father! I'll deal with this poop head!"

Pavel limped as quickly as he could to Menderchuck's aid. Pavel's eyes watered slightly upon seeing Menderchuck, who lay helplessly bleeding on the ground in a puddle of his own blood. In one furious move, Pavel ripped off his own shirt. Menderchuck grimaced while Pavel pressed his shirt down hard upon the gaping wound.

"Torfulson," weakly whispered Menderchuck.

CHAPTER 40: TORFULSON

A cold shiver wracked Menderchuck's body as his severed arm hemorrhaged blood. Sweat poured down Pavel's anguished face while he desperately pressed his blood drenched shirt down onto Menderchuck's gaping wound, forlornly attempting to staunch the bleeding. Several yards away, a slim joyful smile crept onto Duke Belloch's face upon witnessing the sight, then he turned his attention back towards Torfulson.

"Son of Menderchuck?" derisively scoffed Duke Belloch. "Your family has caused me nothing, but trouble. It is time that you die, like your father."

"You first," muttered Torfulson, trying in vain to control his rage.

Duke Belloch raised his blade menacingly and then began to slowly advance. Torfulson stood firm, lifting the blade Arbjak up beside his head, waiting like a poised cobra. The second that the Duke was in range, Torfulson struck with the furious rage that filled every fiber of his being. *CLANG* The sounds of the colliding swords rang out in the din of battle. With a flick of his wrist, the Duke deftly deflected Torfulson's blow.

"Perhaps you should return my guard uniform and let a real man wear it," taunted the Duke.

CLANG Again Torfulson viciously threw

himself into attack. Again the swords clashed violently, and again the Duke effortlessly parried Torfulson's attack.

"Maybe you were adopted," coolly goaded Duke Belloch. "I couldn't have imagined that Menderchuck's son would be such an embarrassing fighter."

CLANG For a third time, Duke Belloch expertly blocked Torfulson's furious attack. Then he made his move. The Duke's sword lunged forward with the expert precision of a lifetime's training towards his opponent's heart.

"AHHHH!" awkward gasped the panicked Torfulson, flinging his blade to the side.

CLANG The two swords met violently. To Duke Belloch's dismay, his sword was deflected from Torfulson's heart, yet it still found purchase in his opponent's arm.

"URGGGH!" gasped Torfulson, feeling the sting of the Duke's blade penetrating his arm's flesh and then its muscle.

With a pained wince and a shudder, Torfulson felt a small warm rivulet of blood begin to pour down his arm as Duke Belloch rapidly pulled his blood covered blade from the punctured arm. Like a flash of lightning, Duke Belloch instantly renewed his attacked, swinging his blade downward towards Torfulson's legs.

CLANG Again, Torfulson swung his sword awkwardly in defense. Again, he blocked the worse of the attack. Again, he felt the sting of steel, but this time in his leg. Gasping in quick pained breathes, Torfulson looked down. There, in the gap of his just cut trousers, he saw the red of blood oozing from his wounded flesh.

"Enough of this game," declared Belloch with a note of finality.

In one swift move, Duke Belloch lunged forward, cutting Torfulson's sword hand.

"AHHH!!!" yelped out Torfulson, dropping Arbjak which clattered to the ground below.

With the fear filled eyes of a hunted rabbit, the bleeding unarmed Torfulson began to stumble backwards as Duke Belloch advanced.

"Do be a good sport, and die quickly," smugly encouraged Duke Belloch. "I have a rebellion to put down."

Duke Belloch lunged forward, aiming to sever Torfulson's head from his body. To the Duke's growing frustration, Torfulson ducked backward in the nick of time, just barely avoiding the attack.

"Hold still," grumbled Duke Belloch through gritted teeth.

Quickening his pace, Duke Belloch charged forward, angrily swinging his sword before him. Tumbling, stumbling, and leaping backwards, the bleeding Torfulson stubbornly kept a hair's breadth ahead of the blade.

"Stop that!" ordered the Duke.

"Too slow old mannn... aHHH!" Torfulson's taunt turned to a cry as his left heel came down awkwardly upon a rock which rolled out from under him.

A look of terror gripped Torfulson's face as his arms flailed about wildly, trying in vain to regain his balance. *THUD* His head bounced violently off of the hard ground as his body toppled helplessly backwards, colliding with the earth below. For a moment, Torfulson's world became a hazy blur, then it slowly returned to focus.

"Wow, there's so many of them," quietly remarked Torfulson to himself, laying upon his back, gazing up at the mass of carrion birds that circled high above.

Torfulson's view of the birds above and the bright blue sky beyond was partially obfuscated as Duke Belloch stepped into view. Like the shadow of death, Duke Belloch hung menacingly over Torfulson, who lay helplessly bleeding upon the ground below.

"You know," coolly began the Duke, raising his sword high above his own head with both hands in preparation for the killing blow. "I really, really can't stand your family. But... I guess that's not going to be a problem for much longer."

The flames of the raging inferno that had once been the grand plantation house reflected their all consuming light off of Belloch's blade. Like chain lightning, the neurons of Torfulson's brain fired in rapid succession, trying desperately to avoid eminent death. And there, in some far off corner of Torfulson's brain, a lonely neuron opened a long shut door, revealing a memory of his father's teachings.

Frantically, fueled by adrenaline and fear, Torfulson kicked his foot upwards as hard as he could into the crotch of Duke Belloch of Rivolli.

"UGHGGH!" gasped the Duke in a high pitched squeal, reflexively releasing the sword which hung above his head.

"OWWWW!" screamed out the Duke as the sword fell, colliding hilt first with his head then bouncing off, landing on the ground beside his feet.

With a great grimace upon his face, a hand upon his crotch, and another hand upon the growing welt on his head; Duke Belloch bent over in great pain. Seizing the moment, Torfulson kicked upward again with all his might.

"Urgggghh," grunt squealed the Duke, puking as he hunched over in pain.

Quickly, Torfulson grabbed a handful of dirt from the ground beside him, then scrambled up to his feet.

"Hey poop head!" shouted Torfulson.

For a moment, Duke Belloch's pained eyes looked up towards Torfulson's voice.

"AGGGGHHH! YOU BASTARD!" cried out the Duke as Torfulson hurled the handful of dirt directly into Belloch's eyes.

Partially blinded by the dirt, doubled over in pain, Duke Belloch stumbled backwards. Suddenly a new bolt of pain ran through the Duke's body as Torfulson kicked him once again in the crotch.

"This is for my father!" defiantly yelled out Torfulson, kicking the Duke's crotch for a fourth and then fifth time. "And this one is for me!"

Face covered in dirt, hands wrapped around his groin, Duke Belloch collapsed to the ground. Writhing in pain and rolling upon the hard ground, Duke Belloch tried in vain to avoid Torfulson's onslaught. Yet no matter how the Duke turned, Torfulson always found some part of the Duke's body to violently kick.

Suddenly, Torfulson felt the surprising touch of a hand upon the back of his neck.

"AH!!! WHAT?! I'm not scared!" screamed out Torfulson, spinning around.

There stood Enok with the mighty blade Arbjak in his hand.

"I think it's time to finish him," suggested Enok, carefully offering the blade to Torfulson.

Torfulson looked at Enok, then at father's blade, then down at the pitiful Duke Belloch. Duke Belloch's soiled faced looked back up at him with tear filled eyes.

"Let me live!" pleaded the Duke through pained breathes. "Please, let me live, and you will never see me again. I will make you rich. I will give you the entire Steppes of Rannsaka. You will be its king."

Torfulson looked down and shook his head slowly.

"I am of clan Chuck as is my father before me," declared Torfulson. "The Steppes know no king. They only know the horse riders of the clans."

Slowly, Torfulson lifted a foot off of the ground. Then, in once swift brutal move, he stomped down with all his weight upon the Duke's neck. *CRAAACK* Duke Belloch's neck snapped like a twig. His eyes rolled back into his head, which then flopped to the side, as his body went limp. Duke Belloch was no more.

"Oh my lords, what the hells man?!" exclaimed Enok in disgust, staring at the mushy pile of blood and bones that had just been Belloch's neck. "That was so brutal. I think I heard every vertebrae break individually. Ewwwww. Next time warn me before you do such a thing!"

CHAPTER 41: ALL GOOD THINGS

The Westernson plantation had changed immensely since the great battle. The dead of the horse clans, and they numbered many, had been lovingly interred in row after row of individual graves that rested peacefully near the shade of the old forest.

Belloch's dead, which included himself and a great multitude of guards and soldiers, lay haphazardly piled in a mass open grave which rested beside 'the pit' in the lee of the burned out husk that had once been the plantation's great house. Daily, for weeks, carrion birds from miles around had grown pleasantly plump, feasting on Belloch's dead.

Torfulson sat nervously upon a makeshift bench which rested in front of one of the many, now spruced up, former slave shacks. Pensively, he gazed towards the plantation's distant great barn and to the ancient oak tree. There, huddled beneath the tree's wide reaching branches, stood the remnants of the horse clans. Hundreds of men, women, and children who were busily brushing down their horses and packing their saddlebags by the light of the rising sun.

"Life is weird," solemnly reflected Torfulson to himself. "A little over a year ago, I was alone in the world, and now I have a giant family."

Torfulson's thought was cut short as the door to the shack beside him creaked open. Out stepped the young 'Old Hag,' who had blessed him long ago.

"Well," she started. "I've done all that I can."

"Will he be ok?" asked Torfulson.

"He won't be winning any rope climbing contests," jested the Old Hag. "But yes, he's fine to ride again."

"Thank you."

The Old Hag nodded, then began to walk away. Torfulson hesitated for a moment, then shouted after her.

"You look beautiful, Old Hag."

For a moment, she stopped, looked over her shoulder at Torfulson, and winked.

"That's more like it. See you around, Torfulson," smiled the young woman as she sauntered off.

Torfulson stood in a momentary daze, watching her wander off. Then he shook his head, coming to his senses, and entered the former slave shack.

The one room shack had changed a lot in the last few weeks. Its walls had been cleaned and painted with a fresh coat of whitewash. A layer of weaved grass mats now covered the dirt floor, and a large bed rested along one wall. There, upon the edge of the bed, sat Menderchuck, who was struggling to put on a shirt with his sole remaining arm.

"Let me help you, Father."

"Oh no," protested Menderchuck. "I can dress myself, thank you. I'm not quite a diaper baby, yet."

"Alright."

"Do you think," asked Menderchuck, gesturing to the empty arm sleeve where his lost arm would have once gone. "Do you think that I'll save a lot of money on shirts now that I can get them half off?"

Menderchuck bellowed in laughter at his own stupid joke while a look of sadness crossed Torfulson's face.

"I'm sorry about your arm, Dad," lamented Torfulson.

Menderchuck smiled brightly back at him.

"It's not your fault, Torf. Don't you worry about it. I'd have traded much more than an arm to have freed our people. I regret nothing. Well... actually, I regret a lot of things. Especially what I had for dinner last night, but I don't regret the arm thing. Great deeds sometimes require great sacrifice."

Torfulson smiled weakly as he heard the door creak open behind him.

"Pavel!" shouted out Menderchuck in joyous

greeting.

Pavel strode boldly into the room.

"So, I hear you're an invalid now," coyly smiled Pavel.

Menderchuck stood up and the two men embraced in a hug.

"Well that proves you are," teased Pavel. "Your hugs are half as weak as they used to be."

"I could still kick your buttocks," retorted Menderchuck in a friendly tone. "So, are you really leaving us? You saved us all, by uniting the clans, and bringing them to our aid in time. You could ride as my third lieutenant."

Pavel shook his head while a tinge of sadness mixed with the joy on his face.

"I did my duty, nothing more," modestly answered Pavel. "And now that my deed is done, I wish to follow my heart. I miss cooking for people and seeing their joy when they eat. With my share of the plantation loot, I've got enough money to start a restaurant of my own. I think I'm going to set up in the city of Miesnatcch, that seems like a good place to dine."

Menderchuck nodded approvingly, gripping Pavel's forearm with his own.

"Well friend," smiled Menderchuck. "If you ever need us, you know where to find us."

"And if you're ever hungry," replied Pavel. "You know where to find me."

Pavel turned and gave Torfulson a goodbye hug.

"I will miss you too, son of Menderchuck," grinned Pavel. "Oh, and keep Muffin safe."

"I will."

Then Pavel walked out of the door and out of their lives.

"Well," began Menderchuck, turning back to Torfulson. "Are the men ready?"

Torfulson nodded. Menderchuck placed his only hand upon Torfulson's shoulder.

"You did good, son. I'm proud of you. Now let's get out of this crap hole."

Father and son walked out of the shack, crossing the plantations grounds towards the mass of horses and riders who waited patiently beneath the great oak tree. As Menderchuck and Torfulson approached the group, the riders silently made way, revealing Enok. Enok stood alone besides the boulder which rested at the base of the old oak tree. His eyes remained fixated upon the great stone, even as Menderchuck stepped up beside him.

"Those etchings," Enok's voice wavered for a moment. "Your son made them for us. They say his name."

Etched upon the stone was the name: "Golgoth."

Reverently, Menderchuck placed his hand upon the boulder.

"Thank you," whispered Menderchuck to the stone.

Enok waited a moment, then cleared his throat, "Chief, we're ready to ride."

Menderchuck composed himself, then looked to Enok, "Well done, you're already making a fine second lieutenant."

Then Menderchuck raised his voice for all to hear, "United clans of the Steppes! We shall never forget what happened here. We shall never forget the blood that was spilled, and the family that we lost. Never again shall we let our division be our downfall, from this day on we are one clan, united. Now mount up!"

"I've been waiting to hear that for a long time," smiled Enok.

"I've specially picked this mount for you, Chief," declared Inju, emerging from the crowd leading a beautiful brown mare.

For a tense moment, Menderchuck circled the horse, judging its merits while Inju nervously watched on. Then Menderchuck gave an approving 'thumbs up' with his only thumb to Inju's great relief.

"Father," started Torfulson, trying to help his father mount the horse. "Let me help..."

"I got this!" refuted Menderchuck, who then tried to leap upon the horse.

Menderchuck slammed awkwardly into the side of the horse, desperately grasping for purchase with his sole hand. Quickly, he slid off, falling to the ground in a cloud of dust. A roar of laughter burst from the untied clan around him. For a moment, sitting upon the hard ground, Menderchuck pouted, but then he too joined in the laughter.

"Fine, fine, help me up," acquiesced the barbarian chief.

Together, Torfulson and Enok helped Menderchuck up off the ground and onto his new horse. Then Enok mounted his horse, and Torfulson mounted Muffin the Slayer of Souls.

"You know what you need?" began Torfulson, sidling his donkey alongside his father's horse.

"A new jerkin?" responded Menderchuck.

"No, you need a mechanical arm."

Menderchuck furrowed his brow, "Oh no, you're not putting one of your contraptions on me."

"No, no, hear me out," protested Torfulson. "I have it all planned out. It'll be way better than the milking contraption was. I'm sure you'll be safe... mostly sure. It'll be great! First, we need to find some gnome sized gears."

Menderchuck smiled, shook his head, then sat up tall upon his horse.

"Sven, where is Sven?!" called out Menderchuck.

"I know a Sven," retorted a voice in the crowd. "It me."

It was Sven. He sat upon a majestic black stallion.

"Yes, yes it is friend," warmly agreed Menderchuck. "Sven, will you do us the honor of taking point and leading the clan westward, toward honor and glory."

"Sure! I like pointing," boldly responded Sven, grabbing his horse's reigns in his hands. "Follow me, clan! To glory and riches! Westward ho!!!!"

Like a bullet, Sven's horse shot eastward towards the blinding morning sun while the rest of the clan sat there upon their horses watching. With a deep sigh, Menderchuck shook his head, then cupped his lone hand around his mouth to yell.

"Sven! Your other West!"

Sven turned his speeding horse in a wide half circle. As Sven and horse darted past the assembled clan he shouted again.

"Westward ho!"

This time the thundering sounds of a multitude of hooves followed Sven's lead as the free untied clans of the Steppes of Rannsaka charged away from the plantation and into the fresh aired dawn of a brand new day.

CHAPTER 42: EPILOGUE

Far far away from the Steppes of Rannsaka, a lone raven silently glided through the clear blue sky. Gently, the bird bent its wings, banking to the right, gliding high above the ancient metropolis of Oppidium. In the city's market district far below, a shocked blacksmith stood in his open air workshop, holding a letter in his calloused hands.

The letter read:

"Dear Blacksmith,

I'm so sorry that I destroyed your prized bellows sometime back. I hope this will make a satisfactory replacement.

My apologies,
~ Torfulson"

A great smile began to form on the blacksmith's face. His eyes remained transfixed upon the massive set of double bellows that rested before him. Their craftsmanship was master grade. Their sides glistened with bands of bronze and steel. They were the largest bellows that the blacksmith had ever seen. Much larger than his old prized ones that had been stolen almost a year before.

"Who cares about my stupid old bellows!" erupted the joyous blacksmith. "These are twice as big. I'm going to make three times as much money with these! Wuuu Hooo!"

THE
END

Thank you for taking the time to read
"The Chains of Belloch."

If you enjoyed it, please consider sharing it
with a friend or leaving a review.
Have a great day!

You can find our other novels and rpg
adventure modules at:

www.zansadventures.com

Made in the USA
Columbia, SC
22 January 2023

10856304R00186